Maisie Frobis.

OFF THE MAP

Liz Hedgecock

WHITE
RHINO
BOOKS

Copyright © Liz Hedgecock, 2020

All rights reserved. Apart from any use permitted under UK copyright law, no part of this publication may be reproduced, stored in a retrieval system, or transmitted, in any form or by any means, electronic, mechanical, photocopying, recording or otherwise, without the prior written permission of the copyright owner.

This is a work of fiction. Names, characters, businesses, places, events and incidents are either the products of the author's imagination or used in a fictitious manner. Any resemblance to actual persons, living or dead, or actual events is purely coincidental.

ISBN-13: 979-8614246112

*For Isabella Bird (1831-1904)
explorer, writer, photographer and naturalist*

CHAPTER 1

The Times, 17th October 1893

LADY EXPLORER MISSING, FEARED DEAD
Lost on board ship bound for Bombay

Miss Charlotte Jeroboam, the well-known lady explorer, has been lost at sea.

Miss Jeroboam was on board the SS Britannia, bound for Bombay, and fell overboard on the evening of October 9th. The ship was many miles from land at the time.

Unfortunately no-one was in the immediate vicinity, and despite the efforts of the crew, Miss Jeroboam could not be rescued.

The captain of the vessel, Samuel Carstairs, who has commanded the Britannia since its launch in 1887, has expressed his deep sorrow at the occurrence, and assured us that all the normal safety precautions were taken on board ship. He describes the event as an unlucky accident.

Miss Jeroboam was on her way to begin an expedition into the jungle of India, where she had been commissioned to collect flora and fauna. Sir Joseph Smith, chairman of the Royal Geographical Society, gave this tribute: 'Miss Jeroboam was a valuable contributor to our knowledge of the further reaches of the Empire. She will be very sadly missed.'

Miss Jeroboam was the youngest of five siblings, and grew up in Cumberland. Her family has been informed, and has requested to be allowed to grieve in private.

***

Maisie Frobisher smoothed her crumpled skirts as best she could and paid the rickshaw runner, not without misgivings that she had been taken the long way round Bombay to Government House. She looked up at the spreading building, so different from its British equivalent, and tried not to feel overwhelmed. Then she consulted her watch. 'Good heavens!' she cried, and hurried up the long flight of steps to the entrance.

She was not the only person hurrying. Several rickshaws had got in a tangle near the entrance, while men in full formal dress were hurriedly dismounting from horses and paying grooms to take them to the stables. All in all, it wasn't quite the well-managed affair that Maisie had expected.

She reached the top of the steps and handed her light shawl to an attendant, who gave her a token in return and inspected her card. 'Through the arch, ma'am, and someone will take you into the reception.' He indicated the way delicately.

Was she mistaken, or was that Mrs Jennings's back view disappearing ahead of her? It was too warm to catch the figure up, but at least it was cooler than the villainous heat of the afternoon, when Maisie had felt equal to nothing except lying on her bed fanning herself and drinking iced water. 'How do people live here?' she muttered to herself.

Once inside the building Maisie was confronted by a hallway and a line of men in tailcoats, each with a welcoming yet quizzical smile on his face. She approached the nearest unoccupied one. 'Miss Maisie Frobisher,' she said, displaying her card.

He scrutinised it without taking it. 'Good evening, Miss Frobisher,' he said. 'I am Captain Hanson, one of the governor's aides-de-camp.' Then he extended a hand. 'Delighted to make your acquaintance.' He bowed slightly and Maisie half-curtsied. The captain took her arm and escorted her into a large, white, reassuringly grand room, weaving expertly between the various knots of people. Here and there Maisie recognised a face she knew; the woman who had sneered over her when she was taken ill on board ship, the eager young man who had almost danced her off her feet, and could that be Colonel and Mrs Fortescue in the corner?

'It seems busy,' Maisie volunteered to her companion.

'Oh, it is,' he said, the smile not leaving his face. 'Half the town turns out to see its new set of arrivals. Can you spot the old hands?' He hailed a waiter who handed him two glasses of champagne, one of which he gave to Maisie.

Maisie sipped while her eyes roved around the room. She began by looking for the people she recognised, and seeking differences between them and the others. The men were useless in that respect, since everyone was in near-identical evening dress. As for the women... Every lady whose face she knew was arrayed in her best. Silks and satins abounded, and diamonds and other jewels winked and twinkled at ears and throat. But each of these ladies was a bright butterfly perched on a bough of blossom, for all the other women in the room were wearing pale muslins. Some were pink, some powder-blue, some primrose yellow, but white predominated; the dazzling, spotless white of a dress painstakingly laundered by someone other than the wearer, put on not more than a few minutes before the wearer is due to leave, and conveyed in a spacious carriage, not a cramped rickshaw.

'The ladies in muslin?' she asked; and it was not really a question.

The aide-de-camp laughed. 'You are very clever, Miss —'

'Miss Frobisher,' Maisie supplied, and drank some more from her glass.

A gentle hand touched her elbow, and Maisie turned to find Sophia Jennings standing next to her, with Mr Merritt a step behind. 'I am so glad to see a friendly face,' she said. 'It feels like an age since we last met, Miss Frobisher.'

'I thought we agreed that we would be Sophia and Maisie from now on,' Maisie replied, administering a light tap with her fan, then opening and making good use of it.

Sophia looked penitent. 'I forgot. I think I am rather overawed,' she said, gazing wide-eyed around the room.

'I am sure they were all in the same position once,' remarked her fiancé.

'As you have found friends,' said Captain Hanson, 'I suppose I had better resume my duties.' He bowed again, appeared about to click his heels together, and departed, setting his empty champagne glass on a tray as he glided past the waiter.

'I wonder if they wind him up and set him going first thing in the morning,' said Maisie, and Sophia giggled. 'Enough of him. How are you liking Bombay?'

'It's . . . interesting,' said Sophia. 'And also expensive. Mother and I were looking for a little bungalow to rent, where I can live too until Christopher and I are married.' She used Mr Merritt's first name quite easily, almost as if she were used to it. 'It is not that the houses are so expensive, it is more the servants. Mother thought she could manage with a cook and a maid, but it appears that isn't the done thing. You need all sorts of servants, far more than in England — a water-carrier, and a sweeper, and I don't know what else — and there is no such thing as a boy-of-all-work, they only do their own job. So Mother and I will have to remain with her friend for the time being.' She made a rueful face.

'Oh dear,' said Maisie. 'In that case, I shall continue at my hotel. Anything else seems far too much trouble, especially in this heat.'

'Exactly,' said Sophia. 'People come calling at the

hottest time of the day, and we sit there with nothing to say to each other. Mother's friend Mrs Ponsonby says that we shall soon get used to the heat, but I doubt it.'

A trumpet blasted through the buzz of conversation, and a voice rang out. 'Pray silence for His Excellency the Governor of Bombay, Lord Montgomery, and Her Excellency Lady Montgomery!'

'Do we applaud?' asked Sophia.

'I'm not sure,' replied Maisie. A ripple of gentle applause spread from the more seasoned inhabitants of the room, and the newcomers took it up.

A tall, straight-backed man in white tie and tails, with a stately woman in white on his arm, passed into the room, and as if by magic the crowd parted to allow them to pass. An aide-de-camp walked on either side, murmuring. The Montgomerys nodded, smiled, and shook hands with the individuals indicated, sometimes exchanging a few words. Maisie felt Sophia quivering beside her until Christopher Merritt whispered in her ear and made her giggle.

'They probably won't come to us anyway,' said Maisie; but the aide-de-camp next to the governor had spotted her, and advanced the Montgomerys towards them with a purposeful air.

'Allow me to present Miss Maisie Frobisher,' he said.

The governor held out his hand and Maisie took it and curtsied low, hoping that was the right thing to do. When she rose, the governor was regarding her with an amused expression. 'Oh yes, I have heard about you,' he said.

'I hope it was good, Your Excellency,' replied Maisie.

He chuckled. 'I should hardly mention it if it were not!'

The aide-de-camp let out a hearty laugh, and Lady Montgomery likewise extended her hand to be curtsied to. 'Miss Frobisher,' she said, with an air of finality in her tone.

'Your Excellency,' replied Maisie. And that was that. The procession moved on.

Ten or fifteen minutes later a string quartet struck up light music, but no-one made a move to dance. Instead, waiters circulated with trays of very British canapés; little biscuits spread with anchovy paste, delicate vol au vents, and cheese and onion tartlets.

'I take it that means the official business of the evening is over,' said Mr Merritt.

Sophia Jennings looked ready to faint with relief. 'Then I shall find a chair,' she said. 'It is so frightfully hot in here.'

'I think there is a way outside,' said her fiancé. Maisie followed his gaze to the far end of the room where a steady stream of guests were congregating, and attendants held open muslin curtains to allow them to pass through. The group advanced with purpose.

'Pardon me…' An unfamiliar young lady, arrayed in particularly fresh and soft-looking white muslin, touched Maisie's arm. 'Have you come from the *Britannia*? What a terrible business about poor Miss Jeroboam!'

'Yes,' said Maisie. 'It must have been terrible. No one was there when it happened, you see.' The face before her seemed innocent enough; but everyone who had occupied that room with Miss Jeroboam was sworn to secrecy.

'What a horrible way to die,' said the lady, with feeling.

'Just imagine — falling into the sea, so cold, and no land anywhere…'

'I'd rather not think about it,' said Maisie. 'Please excuse me, I feel a little faint.' She hurried after her companions. The servant, tall and immaculate in white robes and a bright turban, bowed as he held the curtain aside, and Maisie passed through with gratitude.

A veranda lay on the other side, much cooler than the reception room, and beyond was the garden. Maisie could hear the faint rustlings and noises of creatures enjoying the evening cool. She hoped that they were small and harmless. Strings of coloured lanterns lit the garden, and the effect was magical.

'How beautiful!' breathed Sophia.

'Would you care to take a turn?' asked Mr Merritt, offering his arm.

'Is it safe?' she asked, gazing up into his face.

'I'll look after you,' he said, and they went down the steps.

'Oh Maisie, would you like to come too?' Sophia called over her shoulder.

Maisie laughed. 'I'll leave you to it.' She leaned on the rail of the veranda and gazed at the garden. Even in the dim light, the bushes blazed with colour.

She felt a slight pressure on the rail, and a noncommittal voice said, 'You do know you'll be bitten to death if you go out there, don't you?'

Maisie smiled. 'You must admit that it is very pretty, though,' she said, turning.

Inspector Hamilton was, as usual, beautifully turned

out. Only the fashionableness of his collar, for one who cared to observe such things, marked him as a recent arrival. 'There is a summerhouse down that path,' he said. 'I can take you, if you wish.'

'That would be delightful,' said Maisie.

They confined themselves to remarks about the garden and the weather until they were inside, with the door closed. 'What a frightful palaver,' said Maisie. 'Is this really necessary?'

'I don't know,' said Inspector Hamilton. 'But I prefer to be on the safe side.'

'How are you finding your work?' asked Maisie.

He made a face. 'Slack,' he said. 'We start at ten and finish at four, and not too much happens in between. After all, one wouldn't want work to get in the way of one's sporting engagements, would one?' He inspected his fingernails. 'Perhaps I am being harsh, for they are not long returned from their summer quarters. Not that it matters, since I am quite taken up with Miss Jeroboam.'

'What's going on there?' asked Maisie.

'Officially, nothing happened,' he replied. 'No document was ever lost, and Miss Jeroboam overbalanced in an unfortunate accident. A paragraph or two has appeared in the newspapers, and the family have been told a story which will enable them to sleep at night.'

'That doesn't sound too difficult,' said Maisie.

'It isn't,' said the inspector. 'But the governor knows the truth, and it has fuelled his concerns about his employees' discretion, which is why I was hired in the first place. As far as anyone knows I am a three-hundred-pound-a-year Indian Civil Service man, shuffling my papers with the best of them.'

'I see,' said Maisie. 'Is that what you had in mind when you came out?'

'No,' said the inspector. 'I —'

The door flew open and a laughing young man escorted a woman inside. 'Oh, frightfully sorry!' he exclaimed, as his eye fell on Maisie and the inspector. 'Are we disturbing you?'

'Not at all,' said the inspector. 'We were just leaving.'

They made small talk on the veranda for a few minutes before Inspector Hamilton excused himself. 'I need to see a man about a horse,' he said, bowed, and went back into the reception.

Presently Maisie was joined by a man in rather tired evening dress; perhaps forty, with round spectacles which gave him an owlish look. 'Delightful evening, what?' he said, offering a hand. 'I don't believe I've had the pleasure.'

'Miss Maisie Frobisher,' Maisie said. His handshake was firm and a little damp.

'Ronald Howarth, Esquire, at your service,' he said briskly. 'Just off the boat?'

'That's right,' said Maisie, smiling. 'I had no idea I was so conspicuous.'

'Oh well…' He tapped the side of his nose. 'Bad business that, with the lady explorer. Very bad.' He paused, and Maisie braced herself for a question. 'Would you like a drink?'

She almost sighed with relief. 'Just some water or

lemonade, please.'

'Nonsense! You must try the fruit cup,' he said, and disappeared. When he returned Maisie pronounced her drink very nice, while contriving to take small sips and dispose of the rest in a nearby plant pot when Mr Howarth wasn't looking.

A bell rang, and a shout of 'Carriages!' went up.

'We'd better go in,' said Mr Howarth. 'Nice to meet you, Miss, er —'

'Frobisher,' Maisie supplied.

People were gathering at the far end of the room, and Maisie saw Their Excellencies on the dais. 'Ready to pass you all out and say a word,' said Mr Howarth. He escorted her to the throng. 'Did you come with anybody?'

'No, I came alone,' said Maisie. 'Can I take a rickshaw from here?'

'Of course you can!' said Mr Howarth, in a tone of surprise. He bowed, and was gone.

Maisie queued obediently, shook hands, curtsied and went to hand her token to the attendant. She received her shawl neatly folded, with an envelope and a business card on top.

'There must be some mistake,' she said, 'I didn't —'

'No mistake, madam,' said the attendant, his eyes already on the next person.

A line of rickshaws waited at the foot of the steps. Maisie walked to the first, and got in. *At least I don't have to worry about creasing my dress now*, she thought. *Although what Ruth will say...*

At the hotel Maisie locked the door behind her before

opening the envelope. Inside was a thick printed card, headed *An Invitation*.

You are invited to dine with the Governor
Thursday 19th October, Government House, Bombay

'Two days,' Maisie murmured.

Drinks at 7.30pm for dinner at 8pm
Carriages at 10.30pm
Evening dress
RSVP

Beneath, in black ink, someone had written: *White muslin, please.*

Maisie snorted, and looked at the business card.

Mr Beaumont, British Tailor
Outfitters to Discerning Memsahibs
The Row, Bombay
Express Service Available

'The cheek,' muttered Maisie. 'As if my dresses weren't as good as plain muslin!' But she smiled as she laid the invitation and card on her dressing table, and went to enjoy the hotel garden.

CHAPTER 2

I must go to bed earlier was Maisie's first thought on waking. The day was beginning to heat up already. She dressed hurriedly, so that she could breakfast on the veranda and watch the world go by before the heat became oppressive. Then her eye fell on the business card. She pondered, and picked it up.

'Oh yes,' the chubby little concierge assured her, 'Madame Beaumont's will definitely be open. Shall I summon a rickshaw?'

'Yes please,' said Maisie, 'but isn't it Mr Beaumont?'

The concierge leaned forward confidentially. 'Not really,' he murmured.

The Row turned out to be a row of shops with pretensions to grandeur, but peeling as to paint. *BEAUMONT: BRITISH TAILOR* shouted in gold from one slightly better-maintained frontage, and Maisie entered.

A faint 'Good morning' came from the back of the shop, and a slight man with centre-parted hair and striped trousers advanced towards her. Before he could reach her, though, he was overtaken by a large woman head-to-toe in peach ruffles.

'Good morning, madam,' she said, bearing down on Maisie. 'What can we do for you today?'

'I need a white muslin for dinner at the governor's house,' said Maisie, rather taken aback.

'Very good,' said the presumed Mrs Beaumont. 'When is the dinner, madam?'

'Tomorrow evening,' said Maisie.

'Veeery good.' Mrs Beaumont turned to the back of the shop. 'Hannah, bring the measure!' And then, in honeyed tones, 'If you would step this way, madam.'

Feeling dazed, Maisie followed Mrs Beaumont behind the curtain, where a young Indian woman in a rose-printed muslin appeared presently with a tape measure. All the measurements Maisie could think of, and some that had never occurred to her, were taken and written in a little book. 'Good, good,' said Mrs Beaumont. 'Hannah, bring the muslins.'

Five different bolts of muslin were laid on the counter, and Maisie could see no difference between them. 'Which would you recommend?' she said at last.

'This one is super-fine,' said Mrs Beaumont, laying a finger on the bolt at the right-hand end. 'This one,' — she poked the middle bolt — 'is almost as fine and wears better. Much more practical for dancing and picnics and elephant rides.'

'I hadn't considered the elephant rides,' said Maisie. 'This muslin, then.'

'A very good choice, madam,' purred Mrs Beaumont. 'Will you send someone to pick up your dress, or shall we send it to you?'

'Could you send it to the Hotel Victoria, please,' said Maisie.

Mrs Beaumont inclined her head. 'It will be with you tomorrow, in good time.' She picked up the bolt of muslin and laid it in Hannah's arms, and Hannah scurried into the back of the shop.

I wish dresses were always as easy to arrange, thought Maisie, as she settled herself in a rickshaw. A smile curved her lips as she wondered what sort of parcel would be delivered to her the next day. Presumably it would be a dress such as the discerning memsahibs wore. *I must assume my uniform*, she thought, and her smile broadened. For however uniform Maisie might appear on the outside, she had no intention of conforming within.

***

Back at the hotel Maisie ordered coffee, fruit and toast, and took a seat on the veranda. The day had begun in earnest, and the servants were watering the garden, trimming the plants, and gathering mangoes.

A waiter brought her tray, and laid a newspaper beside it.

'Oh, thank you,' said Maisie. No one else was breakfasting, and so she could read without being thought rude. She opened the newspaper. *The Bombay Telegraph* was printed at the top in Gothic lettering, with *Bombay's*

Most Accurate and Distinguished Daily Newspaper printed underneath, in smaller type. 'I'll be the judge of that,' murmured Maisie, as she turned the pages.

Much of the paper seemed to be working for the Indian Civil Service, as several lengthy articles detailed the improvements lately made in public buildings, water, and education. There were reviews of plays and concerts, including entertainments put on by British amateurs, and reviews of new books with local interest — or not, since a sizeable portion were monographs written by the governor's staff.

If all the information I had on India was this newspaper, thought Maisie, *I wouldn't think that any Indians lived here. Only British people.* She watched the gardeners toiling away, chatting to each other in a language — or was it languages? — she couldn't understand, and shivered. Why, she could not say.

She turned the pages, looking for something she could enjoy. Ah, the personals column.

Lost: gold and pearl brooch, on Monday at the Oval. Reward to finder. Please reply to PL.

Seeking a governess for two lively daughters aged seven and five. Accomplishments welcome but not a requirement. Salary on the usual terms. Please apply to Mrs Jarvis, Rhododendron House.

Where are you? My life has lost its sparkle and become flat. I long to drink from you again. Please send word.

Leopard.

'Good heavens — pursued by a leopard!' said Maisie, laughing. 'I wonder who the poor woman is?' She concluded comfortably that such a message would never induce her to respond.

Wanted: good plain English cook for dyspeptic husband. Apply Forrester.

Maisie smiled, imagining a querulous chap, rather like her own father, poking his curry suspiciously with a fork.

Maisie lingered over her breakfast, then read a novel in her room, sustained by iced lemonade. The calling hour came, and she hoped she would not be disturbed; but the gentle knock at her door said otherwise. 'A Colonel and Mrs Fortescue to see you, madam,' said the attendant.

'I'll meet them on the veranda,' said Maisie, and tidied herself hurriedly.

'We won't keep you long,' said Mrs Fortescue, as bright and brisk as ever. 'Alfred and I are organising a picnic in the Hanging Gardens this evening for us shipmates, and we hope you are able to attend.'

'I'd love to,' said Maisie. 'Do I need to bring anything?'

'Just yourself, Miss Frobisher,' said the colonel, rocking on his heels, hands behind his back. 'We'll organise the refreshments.'

I'm sure you will, thought Maisie.

'We thought it would be nice to see everyone before we part ways,' said Mrs Fortescue.

'Why, are people leaving?' cried Maisie.

'Captain Carstairs certainly will be, for the *Britannia* is due to sail in a couple of days. I don't know what the Merritts are doing about a honeymoon, and we are likely to go up country fairly soon. Bombay is all very well, but we prefer things quieter. We can still come in by train.'

'I am sorry to hear that,' said Maisie, 'but as you say, there's always the train. Anyway, I shall be delighted to come tonight. Is there a dress code?'

'Come as you are,' said the colonel, then grinned. 'Within limits.' Maisie giggled, remembering some of the outfits she had appeared in on board ship.

***

The evening was cool enough for Maisie to enjoy her ride through the streets. Bombay was still busy; the street traders were out, and the bazaar was full of delicious smells and snatches of music and chatter, with an occasional shout as someone fancied themselves hard done by.

When the rickshaw drew up at the Hanging Gardens Maisie could see the Fortescues just inside the gate, directing operations. Two attendants were spreading rugs on a convenient patch of lawn, while bottles stood in ice buckets. Mrs and Miss Jennings stood nearby, looking bewildered, and Maisie went over to them.

'I do hope Christopher gets here safely,' said Sophia Jennings, her hands twisting.

'How is he arriving?' asked Maisie.

'On a horse,' said Sophia. 'He says he can ride, but —'

They turned at the sound of approaching hooves.

'Perhaps this is him now,' said Sophia hopefully.

The approaching grey seemed well managed, but the figure on top had dark, not fair hair under his hat. In another minute he had resolved himself into Inspector Hamilton, dressed in breeches, riding boots, and a loose shirt with a cravat. 'Good evening,' he said, dismounting, and one of the attendants came to take his horse.

'Good evening, Hamilton,' said the colonel. 'That's a fine-looking horse you have there.'

'Apparently his name is Horatio, after Nelson,' said the inspector. 'He is docile, and goes well.'

'I hope Christopher's horse is like that,' murmured Sophia to Maisie.

'Er, yes,' said Maisie. For some reason she found it difficult to speak. The inspector reached into his saddlebag and offered an apple to Horatio, whose top lip pulled back in a smile.

'Oh, he's lovely!' exclaimed Sophia.

Just then more hooves approached, rather less orderly than Horatio's, and a stout piebald tacked towards them. Mr Merritt was on top, bareheaded, and yanking at the reins. 'I said stop, darn it!' he cried. Eventually the horse pulled up ten yards beyond them. Mr Merritt attempted to turn it, then said 'Oh, I give up,' and waited for one of the attendants to hold the horse while he dismounted.

'Well, he is here,' said Mrs Jennings, 'and in one piece.'

'Yes,' said Sophia adoringly.

Captain Carstairs arrived somewhat more soberly in a carriage. 'Good evening, everyone,' he said, doffing his hat, and looking so different out of uniform that Maisie barely recognised him. He caught her glance and laughed. 'Yes, I feel rather strange too.'

'And that completes the party,' said Mrs Fortescue.

'Aren't the Smythes coming?' asked Mrs Jennings.

'No,' said Mrs Fortescue. 'I did call, but they had a prior engagement.'

'Oh, that's a pity,' said Mrs Jennings. 'It would have been nice to see them again. Out of finery, I mean.'

Maisie thought back to the evening before. The Smythes had been there; the ambassador in white tie and tails, and Mrs Smythe in — her brow furrowed. In pale-blue muslin. 'How interesting,' she murmured.

'What is?' asked Sophia.

Maisie laughed. 'Oh, nothing. Something I need to ponder, perhaps.'

'Too warm for thinking,' said the colonel firmly. 'Let's take a stroll round the gardens while the picnic is laid out.'

The gardens were much busier than Maisie would have imagined at this time of the evening. Then again, everything in India seemed to run to a different timetable. Families were taking the air, with their servants managing parasols and pushing baby carriages, and couples were strolling arm in arm, whispering and laughing under the soft lights. She noted how many of the young women wore pastel muslin, and made a note, if her dress turned out well, to order more.

Within a few minutes the party had separated into distinct groups. Mrs Jennings and Captain Carstairs walked with the Fortescues, Sophia and Christopher, naturally, walked together, and Maisie found herself with the inspector.

'Are you permitted to be seen with me tonight?' she murmured, then regretted it as his brow lowered.

'I think I am safe enough,' he said, pulling his cap over his eyes. But she noted that he quickened his pace until they were walking alongside the young couple. 'Did you enjoy the reception last night, Miss Jennings?'

Sophia considered her answer. 'Not really,' she said, with a laugh. 'Government House is beautiful, of course, but it was so crowded, and so hot and noisy.'

'It was,' said Maisie. 'I suppose it is one of those things that has to be done.'

'Yes,' said the inspector, 'I think it is. That reminds me, I want to catch the captain before he departs.' Dropping Maisie's arm, he hurried forward.

'He seems rather agitated,' said Sophia. 'Don't you think so, Maisie?'

'I'm not entirely sure,' Maisie replied. She walked beside Sophia, but she and her fiancé were so wrapped up in each other that it was like walking alone. *What was I thinking about Mrs Smythe? Muslin, that was it.* Mrs Smythe had known the muslin dress code, but had not shared that knowledge with anyone else from the captain's table. *She wanted us to be conspicuous*, thought Maisie. *But why?*

'Let's turn round,' said the colonel. 'I'm working up an appetite.' Only then did Maisie realise that she had taken in nothing of her surroundings. She might as well have been strolling in the park at home for all the attention she had paid.

Halfway back she felt a touch on her arm, and looked up to see the inspector. 'Sorry about that,' he said.

'That's quite all right.' said Maisie, clasping her hands behind her. 'You may speak to whomever you please.'

'I see,' he said. Then, raising his voice, 'Might I borrow Miss Frobisher for a moment, Miss Jennings?'

'Of course you may!' said Sophia, beaming, and after that Maisie could not refuse his arm without seeming rude. The inspector slowed his pace until they were some way in the rear of the party.

'I am not sure I like your Bombay manners as well as your shipboard ones, Inspector,' Maisie said in a low voice.

'It's hardly my fault,' said the inspector. 'And plain Mr Hamilton, if you don't mind.'

'Oh yes, I forgot that here you are a civilian,' said Maisie.

'Look, can we just talk to each other?' he said, abruptly. 'There is something I'd like you to do.'

'Mmm,' said Maisie. 'What is it?'

'I assume you've been invited to the governor's dinner tomorrow,' said Inspector Hamilton. 'Could you stick close to Mrs Smythe? I shall be busy playing the good civil servant.'

'Why do you want me to do that?' asked Maisie. 'Surely you don't suspect her of leaking information.'

'No, I don't,' said the inspector, in a careless tone. 'But it would be useful. In fact, it would help me if you spent as much time as possible with her. The Merritts' wedding will happen soon, and that's the sort of occasion where people let their guard down.'

Maisie took her arm away. 'I will not spend my friend's wedding day spying for you, especially since you can't even give me a good reason for doing it!'

'I thought you'd want to be involved,' said the inspector, in an injured tone. 'You were keen enough on board ship.'

'That was different,' said Maisie. 'That was important, but now you're just casting round for things to do. I am not making myself the laughing-stock of Bombay to please your whims.' She quickened her pace and caught up with her friend.

'The exercise seems to have done you good, Miss Frobisher,' observed the colonel. 'Your cheeks are rosy.'

'Are they?' said Maisie. 'Oh dear.'

'You may as well take your exercise while you can, Miss Frobisher,' laughed Mrs Fortescue. 'You'll have plenty of time to play the idle memsahib.'

Maisie laughed, and she hoped that it did not sound as false to the others as it did to her. She sat down on the picnic rug next to Sophia and ate her share of the little samosas and bhajis which the Fortescues said were much harder to procure than a British picnic. But delicious as they were her mouth felt dry, and the ice-cold wine did not refresh her.

She kept herself resolutely turned away from the inspector, who seemed more than happy to converse with Captain Carstairs. *He wouldn't ask the captain to do such a thing*, she thought, nipping off the corner of a samosa. And with that Maisie determined to enjoy herself at the governor's dinner, and to pay as little attention to the

Smythes and Inspector Hamilton as she possibly could. *After all*, she thought, *he doesn't want to be seen talking to me. I shall make his wish come true.* With that settled she chatted gaily to the others, and had a tolerably good time.

CHAPTER 3

'Now off you go, Miss Maisie,' said Ruth, arranging Maisie's skirts carefully around her and closing the carriage door. 'And make sure you have a good time.'

Maisie barely had time to say 'Yes, Ruth,' before the carriage began to move, carrying her away from the hotel and back to Government House.

The dress was a triumph, she knew it. She had summoned Ruth to her suite when the box arrived, and together they had lifted the lid in trepidation. Within lay a frothy confection, soft as a cloud.

'If it looks as nice on as it does in the box, that will be something,' said Ruth, with grudging admiration. 'Let's see.'

Maisie gasped when she saw herself in the mirror. It was some time since she had worn a pure white dress, and the slight bloom she had acquired on board ship suited it remarkably well. The dress was ruffled, but not too much, and a beautiful fit. 'I feel,' she said slowly, 'almost as I did when I came out.'

'And that was a good few years ago, Miss Maisie,' said Ruth.

'Thank you for reminding me,' said Maisie, and returned to admiring herself in the mirror.

So, furnished with a beautiful dress which she knew suited her, shouldn't she have been looking forward to the evening? *At least I won't have to face him on a horse, or in boots and breeches*, Maisie thought. In any case, she meant to ignore Inspector Hamilton as much as possible.

Such pleasant thoughts kept her occupied all the way to Government House where the driver, recommended by the concierge, helped her out with care. Maisie gripped her evening bag as if it were a weapon, and took her time going up the steps. A footman welcomed her at the door, took her card, and led her into a different, smaller reception room which was not as full as Maisie had expected. 'Are there lots of people still to arrive?' she asked.

The footman turned a critical eye on the room. 'Not too many,' he said. 'This is one of the governor's smaller dinners.' Even so, Maisie judged that there must be at least twenty people in the room.

'Aha, Miss Frobisher!' a voice exclaimed, and Maisie spied the bespectacled figure of Mr Howarth making for her. 'May I get you a drink? Champagne, perhaps?'

'A small glass, please,' said Maisie. She had expected Mr Howarth to bring the drink to her, but instead he linked his arm through hers, patted her hand in a fatherly manner, and led her to the drinks table, where a waiter supplied them both.

'So, how do you like Bombay?' he asked, downing half of his glass in one go.

'I have hardly seen enough of it to judge,' laughed Maisie, 'but what I have seen is most interesting.'

'And what have you seen?' he enquired, raising an eyebrow.

'So far, only my hotel, a tailor's shop, and the Hanging Gardens,' she admitted.

'Oh dear,' said Mr Howarth. 'We can do better than that.' He towed Maisie towards a small group of young women. 'Ladies, may I introduce Miss Frobisher. Miss Frobisher, delighted to introduce Miss Pike, Miss Darling, and Miss O'Connor.'

Everyone half-curtseyed to each other and murmured, 'Delighted.' When the middle one straightened, Maisie recognised the young woman who had asked her about Miss Jeroboam at the reception. And she recognised Maisie too, for her cheeks flushed ever so slightly.

'Miss Frobisher is yet to see the sights of Bombay,' said Mr Howarth. 'I am sure that you can more than do the honours in that department.' The young woman on the right giggled. 'Now if you don't mind I shall leave you to chat, for I need to look someone up.' He bowed and threaded his way through the groups, putting a hand on the arm of a lean grey-haired man.

'He seems frightfully busy,' observed Maisie.

'Oh, he is,' said the lady in the middle. 'Mr Howarth,

don't you know, is the glue that keeps the Indian Civil Service from falling apart.' She said it with a straight face, and then Maisie caught the twinkle in her eye. 'I am Julia Darling,' she said. 'Pleased to meet you again.'

'Maisie Frobisher,' said Maisie, giving her hand.

'Are you related to Lord Frobisher?' asked the young woman on the right.

'Yes, I am his daughter,' said Maisie, feeling rather pleased that they had placed her so easily.

In due course she learnt that the other two ladies were Mary Pike and Nora O'Connor, they had all come to India the previous winter, and between them they had turned down several marriage proposals. 'I mean,' said Nora, 'why would I wish to please a husband, and run a household, and have lots of children, when I can enjoy Bombay society much better without them?'

'I don't suppose your mama agrees,' said Julia Darling. 'Whereas mine wants me to hold out for a top man.'

'What is a top man?' asked Maisie.

'You mean you weren't schooled by an elderly memsahib before coming out?' said Mary Pike. 'Why, a man in the Indian Civil Service with a good salary and a pension — a coming man.' She paused. 'A few weeks after we came...' She lowered her voice and leaned in. 'Mr Howarth indicated that he took a considerable interest in me. Oh, I had to make such terrible speeches about affection and duty.'

'Just imagine,' said Nora O'Connor, her eyes wide.

'I just *couldn't* imagine seeing him at the breakfast table every morning, my dear,' Mary said. 'Hence the terrible speeches. Anyway, we must tell you about Bombay. Although I see you have already found Mrs Beaumont.' She gently applied her finger and thumb to a fold of Maisie's sleeve.

The young ladies confided the best places for picnics, the sights she *must* see, and the only way to mount an elephant gracefully. Maisie nodded and smiled, she hoped in the right places; but every so often she found her gaze wandering around the rest of the room, looking for a tall, black-haired figure.

A gong boomed and Captain Hanson came hurrying over. 'Will you allow me to escort you to dinner, Miss Frobisher?' he asked.

'That would be very kind, Captain,' said Maisie, taking his arm with a slight thrill of relief that she would not have to brave the table alone.

The captain led her into a long dining room. The table sparkled with porcelain and crystal, and chandeliers hung overhead, beneath which the red-upholstered chairs seemed to glow. Maisie held her breath as the captain escorted her in. Where would she be placed? She told herself that it didn't matter, but inwardly she felt it did.

Captain Hanson led her further and further up until she was two seats away from the head of the table. 'Here we are!' he exclaimed. 'Safely delivered. Now, we remain standing till the governor arrives. Just so that you know.' He strode off, presumably to gather any waifs and strays.

Maisie sneaked a look at the place card next to hers. *Edward Mandeville, Esquire*, it said. *That's an interesting name*, thought Maisie. Though perhaps he would turn out to be another Mr Howarth when he appeared in the flesh. She straightened her face hastily, for a young, awkward man was approaching and peering at the cards. His flushed cheeks clashed rather with his sandy hair, and he sported a moustache which, in time, might be described as bushy. 'Is this me?' he asked her.

'Only you can answer that,' said Maisie, with commendable gravity.

'Oh jolly good, it is!' He shifted his focus from the place card to her. 'I thought I would be late. Groom did something to my saddle.'

'Oh dear,' said Maisie. 'But at least you weren't late.'

'No, indeed,' he agreed. 'Which is as well, because old Howarth would have given me such a look. He doesn't tell one off, you know, he just gives one a look.'

'I see,' said Maisie. 'So you work for Mr Howarth?'

The young man pulled a face. 'Yes, and he keeps a pretty beady eye on one, I can tell you. In on the stroke of ten, out not a second before four. And I have exams to study for.'

'Good heavens,' said Maisie, trying not to smile.

'I know,' said Edward Mandeville. 'In this climate it's inhumane.'

'The governor is on his way,' Captain Hanson murmured to her, and took up the place on her other side.

The gong boomed again and a voice cried 'All stand for Their Excellencies!', though everyone was already standing.

Maisie risked a glance along the table. She could not see Inspector Hamilton on the opposite side, although the three ladies she had conversed with earlier were giggling with the men placed between them in a way that suggested they knew each other well. Her gaze travelled down further and further —

Maisie almost jumped when she saw him. Inspector Hamilton was placed near the bottom of the table, and while he looked the same as ever above the neck, the evening dress she had seen so many times on board ship had been replaced by clothes which, while perfectly neat and correct, were a pale imitation of their predecessors. He was talking to the young lady next to him, who had clearly sized him up by his suit and placement, and consequently appeared bored.

Inspector Hamilton must have felt her gaze, for he stopped speaking to the young lady, and met Maisie's eyes. Maisie looked away, abashed at his calm expression, and when she did dare to peep he was gazing towards the head of the table, apparently unconscious of her existence.

'Shuffling papers with the best of them', she thought. *Oh dear.* She had heard, but not understood; and now she felt for the Inspector, and the role he was forced to play. But there was no more time to reproach herself, for ringing footsteps indicated that their host was approaching.

CHAPTER 4

Lord and Lady Montgomery swept into the room and advanced to the head of the table, where two servants waited with their chairs already pulled out. The governor nodded to the table and sat down at the same instant as his wife. That was the cue for the whole company to take their seats, which Edward Mandeville did with a fearful amount of scraping and apologising. Captain Hanson, meanwhile, seated himself in one graceful motion and turned to Maisie. 'I hope you will be able to manage our exotic fare, Miss Frobisher,' he said.

Maisie glanced at the menu. Vichyssoise, grilled turbot, roast chicken, lamb cutlets, and spotted dick. The only concession to their surroundings was a mango sorbet. 'I hope I won't find it too spicy,' she said, with a smile.

'Oh no, it won't be spicy,' Edward Mandeville assured her earnestly. 'I once heard the governor say that he couldn't abide spicy food.' He leaned a little closer. 'Digestion,' he murmured. His expression changed as he looked past Maisie, and he appeared rather injured. 'Oh I say, no need to poke fun.'

'I do apologise, Mr Mandeville,' said Captain Hanson, as the soup was placed before them. 'I certainly didn't mean to.'

As predicted by Edward Mandeville, the soup was velvety, smooth, and bland as milk. The governor turned to his right and addressed his neighbour, Mrs Smythe. The table followed suit, and Captain Hanson turned to Maisie. 'I won't ask you how you like Bombay,' he said, 'for I'm sure you have answered that question many times already. Instead I shall ask what your purpose is in coming here. If it is to catch a husband, you are a little out of season.'

'To be quite honest,' said Maisie, 'I am in Bombay because I wanted to go somewhere different from England.' She looked at her spoonful of soup with a rueful face.

'Ah,' said the captain. 'If you want to go somewhere different then I fear Bombay, or Calcutta, or any Indian city at all is not the best place for you.'

'I seem to be thwarted at every turn,' said Maisie. 'The only place I have seen since leaving England is Marseille, for an afternoon. We could not stop for the Pyramids, and I was ill at Aden. So I desperately need to catch up on my sightseeing. However, I have met some charming ladies who I believe plan to educate me in that respect.'

'Oh, so you have met the Darlings?'

'Is that what you call them?' asked Maisie, laughing.

'Oh, everyone does,' said the captain. 'That or the three witches, depending on how one is treated by them at any given time.'

'I see,' said Maisie, and applied herself to her soup, feeling injured on the Darlings' behalf.

The soup was taken away and the turbot brought, and the governor turned to his other side, so the table did too. 'How long have you been in India, Mr Mandeville?' asked Maisie.

'Oh, quite a long time,' said Mr Mandeville. 'Almost six months.'

'And do you like it?'

'I don't *not* like it,' said Mr Mandeville. 'I suppose it isn't what I thought it would be. I always knew I'd come out. I was in India till I was five, you see, and then I went to England for school. After Oxford I sat the Service exams, then two more years of cramming and, well, here I am. I hoped I'd be with Pa in Calcutta, but Bombay came up and Ma thought it would be good for me to strike out on my own, so to speak.' He paused and blushed again, as if embarrassed that he had said so much in one go.

'So how is it not what you thought?' asked Maisie.

'The thing is,' said Mr Mandeville, 'I was always top dog at school academically, so to speak, and I made sure to fit in a bit of Sanskrit and Hebrew at university, because I thought it would be useful. You know, around the classics.'

'Oh, indeed,' said Maisie, who much preferred to read her Homer and Virgil in translation.

'But Hebrew and Sanskrit aren't much like Hindustani and Gujarati, and then there's the geography and the local bigwigs and their foibles to learn, and that's far worse than *amo amas amat.*' Mr Mandeville realised what he had said, dropped his fork, and clapped a hand to his mouth. 'I'm so sorry, Miss, er —'

'It's quite all right,' said Maisie.

The young man blushed harder, and attacked his fish as if he bore a personal grudge towards it. Maisie turned to her own fish, which was nicely done in parsley butter, but without a hint of spice anywhere. *Is this an omen of my life in Bombay,* she thought. *Exotic on the surface, but bland beneath?*

'I'm being terribly rude, Miss, um —' Mr Mandeville peered at her place card. 'Miss Frobisher.' He smiled at having got her name right, a boyish grin which made him look both considerably handsomer and absurdly young. 'How are you liking Bombay? I assume you're new.'

Maisie burst out laughing. 'If I had a guinea for every time someone has asked me that question, I could go round the world!' She imagined herself on an endless journey of boats and trains and carriages, never stopping long enough to understand any place, but constantly being asked how she liked it. The thought of it, combined with Mr Mandeville's bewildered expression, made her giggle even more.

'I'm sorry, did I say something funny?' he asked.

Maisie got herself under control and sipped some water. Apart from anything else, she was fairly sure that red-faced merriment and white muslin would not make a good pairing.

Maisie re-addressed her fish, as she could see that most

people had finished, and jumped when Edward Mandeville asked, suddenly, 'Were you on the *Britannia*?'

Maisie felt her shoulders stiffening, and did her best to appear relaxed. 'Yes, I was,' she answered.

'What a pity about Miss Jeroboam,' said Mr Mandeville. 'Did you meet her on board the ship?'

Now was Maisie's chance to say that no, she had barely spoken to Miss Jeroboam. 'I did,' she said. 'We sat at the same table for meals, and I walked with her a few times. She was charming.'

'And knowledgeable, I am sure,' said Edward Mandeville.

'I am sure she was,' said Maisie, 'but she wore her scholarship very lightly.'

'How fortunate you were to meet her before —' Mr Mandeville swallowed. 'I hoped to meet her when she arrived and ask her all about her discoveries. I have read of them in the Royal Geographical Society's papers, of course, but it is not the same as speaking to the person who found them.'

'No,' said Maisie. 'And now she has gone.' They finished the fish in silence.

The chicken came, and with it light conversation with Captain Hanson. Beyond him, the governor was conversing with Mrs Smythe again. 'I understand you travelled with Miss Frobisher,' he said, nodding in Maisie's direction.

'Yes, we did,' said Mrs Smythe, 'and many other people besides. Apart from the usual storms in Biscay, it was a smooth passage. Which boat do you normally travel by, Your Excellency?'

The governor began a discourse on his various voyages between this or that governorship, and Maisie refocused on what Captain Hanson was saying. Inside, though, she felt rather heated. *So that's how it is*, she thought. *If it wasn't for me — and the inspector, of course — the Smythes would be in no end of trouble, and she shuns me as an embarrassing reminder.* Maisie stabbed a potato so hard that it almost slid off her plate. She secured it hastily and popped a piece into her mouth to keep her from saying something she might regret in polite company. As for the muslin — now she understood. What better way to demonstrate that the Smythes belonged and the rest of their shipmates did not?

'Are you all right, Miss Frobisher?' enquired Captain Hanson. 'You seem miles away.'

'I do apologise,' said Maisie. 'I was . . . remembering.' *You had better pay attention*, she told herself, *or you will gain a reputation for being inattentive, or possibly strange.*

The rest of the meal passed without event till the governor stood up, and the men followed. Lady Montgomery led the ladies to a chintzy drawing room where coffee and petit fours were served, and Maisie was immediately claimed by the Darlings. 'We shall arrange an elephant ride for you tomorrow,' said Mary Pike. 'In the evening, so that it is not too hot.' She cast an eye over Maisie's dress. 'As it is your first time you may want to wear something a little less fine, just in case. But we shall do our best to see that you get a docile beast.'

As it turned out, ladies and gentlemen were not separated long, and everyone reconvened in the first reception room. Maisie made a point of going up to Mrs Smythe. 'My dear Mrs Smythe,' she said, extending a hand, 'I am so sorry that we have not been able to meet until now.'

Mrs Smythe shook Maisie's hand with a face of stone. 'Yes, we have been so terribly busy,' she said. 'As the new Secretary David has had to meet simply *everyone*, and of course as his wife I have to accompany him. It is the diplomatic life, I am afraid. Oh, there is Mrs Bethune, I really must have a word. Do excuse me.' And off she swept. Maisie could have laughed. *Am I so dangerous?*

'There you are!' exclaimed Mr Mandeville, hurrying over. 'I was looking for you. It's so much easier to chat to people when one is not at dinner. All that turning from side to side addles the brain, I am sure of it.'

'Perhaps you are right,' said Maisie.

'Now where did you slip off to?' asked Julia Darling, slipping her own arm through Maisie's. 'Carriages will be here soon, and you have not told us how to find you.'

'I am at the Hotel Victoria,' said Maisie.

'Then I shall send you a note there tomorrow, as soon as I have arranged the elephant ride.'

'An elephant ride?' said Mr Mandeville. 'How topping! May I come? I mean, that is, if it would be all right, you know…'

'The more the merrier, Mr Mandeville,' said Julia Darling, with a twinkle in her eye. 'We thought of asking two or three of the young men, so if you would oblige I'll get someone to run a message to your office tomorrow.'

Edward Mandeville blushed and stammered his thanks,

and as he did so Maisie's gaze roamed round the room. Inspector Hamilton was being talked at in a corner by a man in similar dress to his own, presumably a colleague. Then her eyes met Mr Howarth's. He jerked his head away and walked towards the door.

What was that for? thought Maisie. Then she remembered Edward Mandeville's complaints about 'old Howarth', and smiled. He was probably keeping an eye on his charge. She caught the sound of her own name, and hastily returned to the present. 'I beg your pardon?'

'I said we shall probably ride out at six,' replied Nora O'Connor. 'So tell your young men half past five, Mr Mandeville. I know what you're like for punctuality.'

Mr Mandeville blushed again, and launched into an indignant defence of the service as a whole. Julia Darling caught Maisie's eye, and winked.

Maisie reviewed the evening as her carriage sped along the quiet streets of Bombay. She had met new people, and made friends; she was going on an elephant ride tomorrow; and she had managed to annoy Mrs Smythe in public. All in all, not a bad night's work. Then the image of Inspector Hamilton sitting at the foot of the table, ignored by his dinner partner, floated into her mind. She tried to push it away, but it would not go. *I began the evening so determined to ignore him and have fun*, she thought. *And I did.* But she would have preferred the righteous anger she had felt on the way to dinner to the embarrassed sympathy she felt now.

CHAPTER 5

Maisie walked slowly towards the elephant, who, if she were not mistaken, had an evil glint in his eye.

'Don't worry,' called Julia Darling. 'He's a softy really. He can't help his expression, can you Rajah?'

The mahout said something to Rajah, and the elephant lay down, the howdah on his back wobbling in what seemed to Maisie rather a dangerous manner. The mahout moved close to his side and knelt, his hands clasped in a makeshift stirrup. 'Come on, Missy Sahib, right foot here,' he said, in heavily accented English. 'One-two-three-up!'

'Like the man says,' said Mr Dawlish, who was lounging against a tree, hands in pockets.

'I don't see why I have to go first,' said Maisie, stopping perhaps five feet from the elephant.

'You'll be fine,' said Nora O'Connor, 'just remember what we told you.'

Maisie sighed, and took the last few steps. After all, an elephant was not so much bigger than a horse, and it wasn't as if she had to control Rajah, for her mahout would do the steering. 'Here goes,' she said, putting her right foot gingerly on the mahout's clasped hands, and her hand on his shoulder.

'That's it, Missy!' he cried. 'When I say up, grab that pole.' He jerked his head at the corner post of the howdah, which looked impossibly far away. Maisie swallowed. 'One-two-three-up!'

Maisie felt herself shoot sharply upwards. Her gaze was fixed on the approaching corner post, and she stretched both hands to it. One hand caught; one did not.

'Quick!' shouted the mahout.

Maisie let out a very unladylike grunt and swung her other hand up, then gripped the edge of the howdah and walked her feet up Rajah's side, hanging on for dear life, until she threw herself inside the howdah panting.

Cheers and applause came from the spectators, and she waved a feeble hand.

'Hold on,' cried the mahout. 'Once I am on board, Rajah will stand.'

Maisie flung out an arm and clutched the post of the howdah. A few moments later the world lurched backwards, then to the left, then right, and suddenly she was higher in the air than she had ever thought possible. She risked a peep over the side, and her stomach lurched more violently than the elephant had.

'Well done, Miss Frobisher!' shouted Mr Mandeville.

'Thank you,' said Maisie, reflecting that this was

perhaps the most bizarre episode of an unusual day.

It had begun normally enough, with an early awakening followed by breakfast, or chota hazri as Maisie was learning to call it, on the veranda. The waiter offered her a copy of the *Bombay Telegraph*, and Maisie leafed through it idly as she drank her coffee and nibbled on slices of mango. More achievements, more glowing reviews….

A piece of mango went down the wrong way, and Maisie burst into a violent fit of coughing.

Where are you, my dear one, my tonic and stimulant? Where do you hide? Perhaps your friend can tell me, the one who is so pretty in her new white muslin. You should ask her to speak with me. Leopard

Maisie stared at the paper. *There must be thousands of women wearing white muslin in Bombay*, she thought. *Why should it be me?* She closed the paper and returned to her breakfast; but the mango which was so sweet and delicious before now seemed sickly. She ate a piece of dry toast to steady herself. *It means nothing*, she told herself. *Just silliness*. And with that she took the newspaper to her room, and shut it in the drawer.

She was thankful that today she was visiting Beaumont's with Miss Jennings. The carriage was ordered as the best way for two to travel in comfort, and when she drew up to Mrs Ponsonby's house Miss Jennings was already waiting outside, looking anxious under a parasol.

'Are you sure it will not be expensive?' she asked.

'My bill was very reasonable,' Maisie assured her. 'In

any case, I mean to make you a present of the dress.'

'You don't have to do that,' said Sophia Jennings quietly. 'Mother and I can manage. She did recover some of her money.'

'That isn't the point,' said Maisie. 'I must buy you a wedding present, and this is something practical that you will be able to wear for your wedding, if you like, and afterwards too.' *And you will get on much better in Bombay wearing it than you will in the dress you have on*, she added to herself.

Miss Jennings fretted while she was greeted, and measured; and yet once the bolts of muslin had been brought, and she had fingered them, and been assured of the price per yard and the price once made up, a shy smile stole over her face, and Maisie knew that the battle was won.

'Ordinary or express service, madam?' Mrs Beaumont asked Maisie.

'Express, please,' said Maisie firmly. 'And while I am here, please could you make me three more dresses similar to this one, in white, lilac, and pink.'

Mrs Beaumont's eyes gleamed. 'Express service, madam?'

'Most definitely,' replied Maisie.

Miss Jennings, full of praise and thanks, invited Maisie to Mrs Ponsonby's bungalow for a cup of tea, and Maisie submitted to being cross-examined by her host, who seemed rather suspicious of her. *Yes*, thought Maisie, stifling a smile, *I am clearly more dangerous than a tiger loose in the bazaar.*

She had taken a nap in the afternoon to be fresh for the elephant ride. The Darlings' note had said they would pick her up from the hotel, and it was nice not to have to arrange a rickshaw or carriage, or indeed know where she was going. The Darlings arrived on time, a little cramped in their carriage, and Maisie squeezed in with difficulty, thankful that her new dresses would arrive before she had to attend any more social functions.

They drove to the elephant stable, or at least Maisie supposed that was what you called it, and found three young men already waiting for them. Mr Mandeville doffed his hat. 'Allow me to introduce Mr Dawlish and Mr Marshall, also of the Indian Civil Service.' The other two young men stepped forward and bowed with a flourish of their caps.

'Have you arranged the elephants?' asked Mary Pike.

'Why, I thought you were doing that,' said Mr Mandeville.

'Call yourself an administrator,' she snorted, and Julia and Nora giggled.

They chatted desultorily while the elephants were brought out and judged. 'Could you not have found a fourth?' asked Julia Darling. 'Then we would be an even number.'

'Well, not everyone was in,' protested Mr Mandeville. 'A lot of chaps had to go up country. There's been a bit of bother a few miles north. The only chaps left at work apart from us were old Howarth and a new boy. And I couldn't ask *him*.'

'Why not?' asked Julia.

'Slogger,' said Edward Mandeville with a wrinkle of his nose, and Maisie thought of his classics degree from Oxford, and his extra classes in Sanskrit and Hebrew. 'A nose-to-the-ledger sort of chap. I didn't think you'd like him.'

'Does he have an unfortunate manner?' asked Nora O'Connor.

'Oh no, he seems quite pleasant,' said Edward Mandeville, 'and he comes for a peg and stands his round with the rest of us. But I don't like the cut of his waistcoat, if you know what I mean.'

'Maybe you should have asked him anyway, and let us be the judges,' said Maisie.

'Perhaps,' said Edward Mandeville carelessly. 'But I didn't think it was proper to ask a chap I barely know to socialise with young ladies.' A trumpet from the stable ended the conversation.

It took fully half an hour for everyone to be seated on an elephant, during which time Maisie had recovered herself enough to sit up, look about her (although the first glimpse of the ground below was terrifying) and even exchange a few words with the others; but she did not let go of the howdah for an instant.

'I will take you to Sewri Hill,' shouted the mahout. 'That is two miles, and a good place to picnic. You may see flamingoes.'

Maisie felt a little seasick as the howdah tilted first on one side, then on the other; but she reflected that it was nowhere near as bad as traversing the Bay of Biscay, and kept her eyes fixed on the mahout's back. She could hear the shouts and laughter of the others. *I shall join in once I am safely on the ground*, she said to herself.

At length Rajah stopped. 'Hold on,' called the mahout, and barked an order to Rajah, who knelt with such alacrity that Maisie nearly slid out of the howdah altogether. 'You can dismount now, Missy Sahib.'

Getting down was much easier than getting up, and Maisie managed to land on both feet. 'Bravo, Miss Frobisher!' cried Mr Mandeville, who looked rather green, but the others appeared as cheerful as if they had just disembarked from an omnibus.

Sadly no flamingoes were visible; for they had taken so long to reach the picnic spot that it was almost dark save for the mahouts' lanterns. The picnic was spread from a basket which said *Fortnum & Mason,* and Maisie nibbled on a dry cracker while listening to the men gossiping. *And they say women chatter*, she thought resentfully. The office formed a large part of their discourse, but billiards and taverns and bets were discussed too. 'Did you see that game I won against Hamilton the other day?' asked Mr Dawlish. 'I took a few rupees off him that night, I can tell you. He looked quite sore about it.'

'Maybe he's short of cash,' said Mr Marshall. 'Furlough can be expensive, I believe. I wonder where he was stationed before he went on leave.'

'In a hill station, perhaps,' said Mr Mandeville.

'He told me he'd been in Madras,' said Mr Dawlish. 'That explains his lack of Hindustani. And he does things in a funny way. Not our way.'

'Dead men's shoes,' said Mr Mandeville gloomily, and

ate a finger sandwich in two bites.

They packed up the picnic and Maisie discovered that mounting an elephant was much easier the second time you did it. She could even watch the others getting aboard, which they did with a great deal of laughter and teasing. She had stuck to plain fare in mind of the ride home, but the lurching of the ride out was now a gentle swaying, as if she were in an enormous gilded cradle. Her eyes closed . . . and she jumped awake at a yell followed closely by a crash. Rajah stopped. 'What's happened?' cried Maisie, looking out into the night.

'Mandeville's had a tumble,' said Mr Marshall laconically. 'His elephant has taken offence and burst his straps.'

Sure enough, a howdah with a broken side was lying on the ground, and Mr Mandeville crawled from the wreckage, apparently not much the worse for his ordeal. 'Damn elephants!' he cried, kicking the howdah. 'Why do they take against me so?'

'Maybe they don't like the cut of your waistcoat,' Julia Darling shouted, laughing heartily.

Mr Mandeville was admitted into Mr Marshall's howdah and the rest of the journey progressed without incident, till the party shook hands and Maisie climbed back into the Darlings' carriage.

'You look exhausted, Maisie,' said Nora. 'It is like that the first time. I slept until ten after my first elephant ride.'

'I expect I shall do the same,' said Maisie, covering a yawn with her hand. They arrived at her hotel, and she waved goodbye to the Darlings from the top of the steps while the doorman waited patiently.

I shall be so glad to get to sleep, thought Maisie, as she walked down the corridor towards her suite. *I hope Ruth has left my nightgown ready. I won't ring and wake her.* She yawned again, a huge gape which she was glad no one was there to see, and unlocked the door.

How odd, she thought. *I was sure I left the light —*

An arm pinioned her from behind, and another clamped over her open mouth. 'Quiet,' said a low, determined voice. 'Not one word.'

CHAPTER 6

Maisie wriggled as hard as she could, to no avail. *You leave me no choice*, she thought, and bit the hand covering her mouth as hard as she could.

The effect was instantaneous. Inspector Hamilton gasped and loosened his hold immediately. 'What did you do that for?' he asked in an angry whisper.

Maisie snapped the light on and faced him, panting. 'Give me one good reason why I shouldn't scream the place down,' she said. 'How dare you!'

'I didn't have much choice,' said Inspector Hamilton, nursing his hand. Maisie saw a spot of blood on the handkerchief he had pressed to it, and felt no remorse at all.

'One minute you tell me that we can't possibly be seen in public together, and then you break into my room and — and manhandle me!' He took a step towards her.

'I'm still perfectly capable of screaming,' she said, but her anger was beginning to lessen. 'Why on earth did you do it?'

'Because I need your help,' said the inspector. He sat on the chaise longue, wrapped his handkerchief twice round his hand, and attempted to tie a knot.

'Here, let me do it,' said Maisie. She sat down beside him and unwrapped the handkerchief. 'You ought to wash that.'

'You're probably right,' said the inspector. 'For all I know you could have rabies.'

'Very funny.' Maisie wetted a flannel and gently cleaned the cut, then went to her travelling medicine chest. 'Take a deep breath.'

The inspector winced as she dabbed iodine on the cut, then bandaged it. 'Thank you,' he said, with an effort.

'Would you like some brandy?' asked Maisie. Under the harsh electric light the inspector's face was even paler than usual.

'I'm not an invalid, you know,' he said. 'I just didn't expect you to bite me.'

'Don't attack me in my own room, then,' said Maisie. Suddenly she was conscious of how close together they were, and moved a little further away. 'What do you mean about help?'

'I hope you had a lovely evening with your cronies,' said the inspector. 'I assume they didn't mention the uproar in the office today.'

'Mr Mandeville mentioned a spot of bother,' said Maisie thoughtfully.

The inspector snorted. 'That's an understatement. I wouldn't expect him to grasp the seriousness of the situation. Howarth probably had him copying log tables.'

'He does have a degree from Oxford, you know,' said Maisie.

'That's as may be,' said the inspector. 'It doesn't mean he's got an ounce of common sense.'

Maisie thought about defending Mr Mandeville, but more pressing matters were at hand. 'So what has happened?'

'Howarth was summoned to Government House first thing yesterday,' said the inspector. 'The governor had received a telegram from one of our Maharajahs. Quite apart from being couched in most uncomplimentary terms, he clearly knows something he isn't meant to.'

A wave of nausea swept over Maisie. 'Another information leak?' she asked, quietly.

'It appears so,' said the inspector. 'The governor has been trying to curb the Maharajah's allowances for some time. He has an official in charge of paring away at them gradually, so that the Maharajah wouldn't notice.'

'Why does he make the Maharajah allowances?' asked Maisie.

'To keep him sweet,' said the inspector. 'Bombay is under direct rule, of course, but the Maharajah is held in great reverence, and if his people thought he had been insulted —' He paused. 'Let's just say that the sums involved are probably worth spending.'

'I see,' said Maisie. She shivered.

'So Howarth dispatched a delegation on horseback to

go and calm him down,' said the inspector. 'Meanwhile, he had me poring over the Maharajah's telegram for clues, and matching it to the information in the ledgers. The obvious suspect is the man who was in charge of the penny-pinching; but of course he wouldn't be that stupid. Unless it were Mandeville — but he would be perfectly happy with the status quo, I should think.'

'You really don't like him, do you?' said Maisie.

'No, I don't,' the inspector replied. 'He's a snob and an idiot, and I despised the way he was hanging around you at dinner.'

'Ah,' said Maisie, 'I see.' The inspector glared at her. 'Anyway,' she added hastily, 'why do you need my help? What would I be able to do?'

'I thought you could observe your new friends,' said the inspector. 'Particularly the male friends you have acquired in the civil service. Mandeville doesn't like me, I can see that; but perhaps he will trust you. I suspect he is loose-lipped enough in the presence of a pretty woman.'

'Why thank you, Inspector,' said Maisie. 'I didn't know you cared.'

'I am merely stating a fact,' said the inspector; but the twinkle in his eye suggested a great deal more. He moved closer, and —

'Wait,' said Maisie, suddenly. 'Someone else thinks I'm pretty.'

'I'm sure they do,' murmured the inspector.

'No, I mean — Wait a minute.' Maisie got up, went to the chest of drawers, and retrieved the newspaper. 'At least, it might be me.' She opened the paper to the right page, and pointed. 'If it was just this, I'd think nothing of it, but this "Leopard" has advertised before, and it was such a strange message. Something about sparkle and drinking, and life being flat. And it was addressed to a woman who had disappeared. At first I thought she did not want his attentions; but now I wonder…'

'When was this?' asked the inspector.

'A couple of days ago.'

'I'll find a copy.' He underlined the words of the advertisement with his finger, and Maisie tried not to look at his bandaged hand. 'So you think this might be you? But in that case, who is your friend?'

Maisie felt as if her heart were being squeezed tight. 'The only friend I have who has disappeared is Miss Jeroboam.'

'Jeroboam,' said the inspector, tapping the newspaper. 'A large bottle of wine, often sparkling.' His eyes met Maisie's. 'Good heavens.'

Maisie stared at him. 'What are we going to do?'

'I don't know.' The inspector pushed back his hair. 'Let me think.'

Maisie swallowed. 'We could answer the advertisement,' she said, in a small voice.

Now it was the inspector's turn to stare. 'Do you think that's wise?'

Maisie shrugged. 'Probably not. But if someone who knew Miss Jeroboam wants to speak to me, and information is being leaked, then…'

'But it's incredibly dangerous,' said the inspector. 'Why is it that when I ask you to do a perfectly harmless task you refuse point-blank, and now you're willing to jump head-first into something ten times worse?'

'But you could shadow me,' said Maisie. 'Or one of your colleagues, if you don't care to be seen with me.'

'Do be quiet,' said Inspector Hamilton. 'Of course I'll watch out for you. What should your message be?'

'I have no idea,' said Maisie. She fetched her writing case. How odd that she had been on the verge of falling asleep not half an hour earlier, and now she was wide awake.

'I wish I could speak to my friend, but in her absence I must speak to you,' said the inspector.

Maisie wrote the words down. 'Advise me of time and place,' she said. 'How do I sign it?'

Inspector Hamilton looked at her, and the twinkle had returned. 'Name a small dark animal,' he said. 'Perhaps a monkey?'

'Do you mind?' said Maisie. She thought for a moment, then wrote: *Panther.*

A slow smile curved the inspector's lips. 'If you say so,' he replied. 'You can certainly bite like one.'

'You should see what I do when I'm really annoyed,' said Maisie.

'Is that an invitation?' He moved closer, then checked himself. 'Perhaps not right now. I don't want to lose a hand.' But he said it very softly.

'No one would know,' murmured Maisie.

'We would.' He sighed. 'Besides, I wouldn't want to crease your pretty dress any more than that elephant has done.'

'How did you know about —'

'I have ways.' He took a step back. 'Do you think you could send the message tomorrow morning, to appear the next day?'

'I don't see why not,' said Maisie. 'Will you be prepared?'

'Oh yes,' Inspector Hamilton replied. 'I'm always prepared.' He put a finger to his lips, then leaned forward and touched Maisie's. 'Now get some sleep, young lady, since we both have work to do in the morning.' He got up, opened the door to Maisie's balcony, and was gone.

Maisie sat, her finger touching her mouth, gazing at the message she had written. Part of her looked forward to seeing what tomorrow might bring; but the greater part of her wished that the inspector could have stayed. Eventually she sighed, changed into her nightgown, and lay down beneath her mosquito net; but she lay awake a long time, unable to quell the thoughts racing through her head.

CHAPTER 7

At first Maisie thought she was still dreaming when she opened her eyes. For a moment she could not work out where she was. Then the writing case on her dressing table caught her eye, and she remembered.

How strange, she thought, sitting up in bed and rubbing her eyes. The writing case was still there. Had Inspector Hamilton really been here, too? Maisie went through to her sitting room. There was the chaise longue where they had sat, though now the cushions were as smooth and cool as if no one had ever touched them. 'But he did,' she whispered. She sighed, and picked up the message they had composed together. Then she leafed through the newspaper, found the pricing information for placing a message, and drew the necessary number of rupees from her purse.

'Do I sign it?' she murmured.

It was easy to write *Dear Sirs, Please place the following in the personal column of the Bombay Telegraph, in the next available edition.* Yet Maisie could not bring herself to write her name at the bottom. *If you leave it blank they will be suspicious.* In the end she printed *Miss J Smith*, slid the note and its enclosure into an envelope, and addressed it.

Now for breakfast, she thought.

She read the newspaper on the veranda, as usual, and found another message in the personals section.

I would like to raise a toast to my dear one. Please contact me in haste. Leopard.

Compared to the previous messages, this one was almost curt. Leopard might be losing patience, or on the verge of giving up. Maisie finished her breakfast and took the envelope to the front desk of the hotel, where the concierge was only too happy to give her a detailed account of Indian postal rates, and supply an appropriate stamp.

'Is madame seeking a bungalow to rent?' he asked, looking rather disappointed.

'Oh no,' said Maisie. 'You take care of me so well that I would not dream of leaving. It is merely a minor personal matter.' The use of the word 'personal' was enough to make the concierge stammer a flustered apology and retreat to the back room, leaving Maisie on the verge of giggles.

And now, for the first time, a whole day stretched ahead

of her without an engagement to look forward to. She considered asking the concierge for information on notable buildings she might visit, but she did not wish to prise him from his sanctuary. *I know*, she thought. *I shall pay some calls.* That would be an excellent opportunity to begin her task of discovering more about the Civil Service men. She returned to her room and rummaged in her bag for the cards she had been given. Mary Pike's at-home days were Tuesday and Thursday; Julia Darling's day was Wednesday, but on the back of the card she had scrawled: *You are welcome to pop in any time.* Nora O'Connor's card said *Generally at home, unless I am not.* Today was Saturday. 'It's worth a try,' Maisie said to herself, and summoned Ruth to help her examine the contents of her trunk and choose a dress suitable for visiting.

'When are the new dresses coming?' asked Ruth.

'Later today, I think,' replied Maisie. 'It is strange how quickly one gets used to a new fashion,' she said, holding the yellow silk against her and rejecting it. 'This heat accounts for a great deal.'

'That it does,' said Ruth. 'I swear I was never so warm in my life. But they tell me it will get warmer, and that this is the cool season.' She snorted in disbelief.

'How are you finding India, Ruth?' Maisie asked, feeling guilty that she had not considered her maid's welfare before.

'Tolerable, Miss Maisie, but odd,' said Ruth. 'There is another maid in the hotel and she has taken me under her wing, so to speak, but she won't let me do anything. I said I was going for a walk the other day, and she absolutely refused to let me. Apparently memsahibs don't use their feet.' She chuckled. 'We were passing the bazaar the other day and I saw a stall with lovely silks — I thought they might suit you — and she wouldn't let me out. Apparently the bazaar is not for us, and when I said I could see people shopping in there who definitely weren't Indian, she said they were probably soldiers' wives. Perhaps she was giving herself airs — but I don't know where I am, really.'

'I'm not sure I do,' said Maisie. 'I shall wear my Columbine dress today.' She fingered the material and remembered the last time she had worn it, decorated with patches, at a masked ball. She shuddered slightly, and hoped that today would turn out better than that occasion.

At the appointed hour Maisie bumped through the streets in a rickshaw, gazing at the sights around her. It was a while since she had ventured outside in the heat of the day, and though the streets were still busy everyone seemed to move in slow motion; the water carriers' cries were more lethargic, the donkeys moved more slowly, and a sacred bull ambled down the street, stopping here and there to investigate the food stalls which interested him. A shopkeeper shouted at him, but the bull took no heed and poked his nose further into the shopkeeper's wares.

Julia Darling lived at Hibiscus Lodge, a wide, spreading bungalow on a street just off what the concierge had informed her was one of the best roads in Bombay. The grounds were well-kept, and the bungalow freshly painted. Maisie rang the bell, and waited.

The servant who answered the door took her card, bowed, and withdrew. Maisie heard voices within, and presently he returned. 'This way, please,' he said, stepping outside, and led Maisie round to a veranda at the back of the house, where Julia and Nora were sitting with a pitcher of iced lemonade.

'Good morning, Maisie,' said Julia, indicating a chair. 'I am glad that you came to me, for it is far too hot and I am far too lazy to leave the house today. Have you recovered from your elephant?'

'Elephant? Oh yes!' exclaimed Maisie. So much had happened since then that she could scarcely believe the ride had happened only the evening before. 'I enjoyed it tremendously.'

'I'm not sure you said that at the time,' remarked Nora, and laughed.

'Perhaps not,' said Maisie, laughing too, 'but now I have slept on the experience.'

'And did you enjoy the company?' asked Julia.

'Of course I did,' said Maisie. 'Everyone was very kind — except for making me go first, of course. And everyone seems nice.'

'Including the chaps?' Nora asked, with a sly smile.

'Yes, including the chaps,' said Maisie. 'I hope we shall go on more outings together.'

'Then you are not the only one,' said Nora, and looked so maddeningly secretive that Maisie demanded to know what was behind her expression. 'Shall I tell her?' she asked Julia.

'Oh, I think you should,' said Julia. 'Forewarned is forearmed.'

'Tell me what?'

Nora took her time pouring a glass of lemonade and putting it in front of Maisie. 'A certain young man was singing your praises,' she said. 'Apparently you are a sporting young lady and jolly good fun. As well as being very nice to look at.'

Maisie could feel her face growing warm. 'Really?'

'Yes, really,' said Nora. 'He was so complimentary about you that I grew rather jealous. Of course I promised not to breathe a word, so you know nothing of this.'

'So who said all these lovely things?' asked Maisie.

'You mean you don't know?' said Julia. 'Good heavens, Maisie, I thought you had more sense than that.'

'Maybe I don't wish to guess wrong and embarrass myself,' said Maisie. 'Please put me out of my misery, Nora.'

Nora considered, then relented. 'Edward Mandeville, of course. Not that I needed him to confide in me, for it was written all over his face.' She paused. 'I can see you are not displeased either, Miss Frobisher.'

'Oh no,' said Maisie hastily, her face burning hot. 'But it is rather sudden. I never expected —'

'I blame the heat,' said Julia Darling. 'It does funny things to a man.' She laughed. 'Seriously, Maisie, you could do far worse if you mean to stay here. His father is an important man in Calcutta; a Collector, or a Commissioner, or . . . something beginning with C, I can't quite recall.'

'Is that good?' asked Maisie.

'Of course it's good!' cried Nora.

'So . . . what would you do?' asked Maisie, bewildered.

'Encourage him,' said Julia.

'Be cool towards him,' said Nora.

'You two are no help,' said Maisie.

'In all honesty,' said Nora, 'I would give things a little time. You have scarcely been here two minutes, and Mr Mandeville may adore you from afar for a while. I have seen men absolutely potty about a girl, only to lose their heart to someone else off the boat a month later, and then where are you?'

'Quite,' said Julia.

'Very well,' said Maisie. 'I shall take your sage advice into account. Now let's discuss something else before I melt through embarrassment.'

Maisie returned from a long visit to find Ruth unpacking her new dresses with great care. 'A note came for you, Miss Maisie,' she said, fetching it from the desk and putting it in Maisie's hand.

The note was simply addressed *Maisie*, and she heaved a sigh of relief. She did not know the writing, but she could guess the owner of the slanting, looped hand.

Dear Maisie,

My dress arrived today and it is so beautiful that I don't know how I shall keep from wearing it. Thank you so much! I shall never forget your kindness.

My other good news is that Christopher has obtained a special licence at last, and we are to be married next Saturday, the 28th, in St Saviour's Church, at 9 am. I do hope you will be able to join us.

With love and thanks,

Sophia

Maisie gave the note to Ruth, who read it with a broad smile. 'Just as well you ordered more dresses, Miss Maisie,' she said. 'You are becoming a social butterfly, what with dinners and elephant rides and now a wedding.'

Maisie thought of the conversation she had had not an hour before, and put her hands on her cheeks to cool them. Nora and Julia, while fancying themselves so sharp, were mistaken. They had thought the expression on her face showed mutual attraction between herself and Edward Mandeville, when it was no more than satisfaction that she would be able to spend time with him, and hopefully extract useful information. Then her embarrassment and guilt at the misinterpretation had fuelled the fire. 'It is terribly warm,' she said. 'I might draw the curtains and lie down, Ruth.'

'I knew that going out in the heat today was a bad idea,' said Ruth censoriously. 'Too much excitement.'

She's right, thought Maisie, lying in the darkened room listening to the birds singing outside. *I have had far too much excitement, and if anything it will get worse.* She closed her eyes to shut it out, but so many images crowded in on her that she opened them again. She felt her heart thumping, and her mouth was dry. 'Whatever next?' she whispered.

CHAPTER 8

What happened next was an uneventful Sunday; a service at the British church, no duller than attending in London, followed by a nap and then a drive around Bombay, whose principal interest was in observing all the other identically-dressed British people doing the same thing. Maisie fidgeted in her carriage, and wished the day away.

She had the dubious pleasure of opening the *Bombay Telegraph* on Monday morning and seeing her words reproduced in newsprint. Somehow they looked much more final sandwiched between requests for staff and appeals for the return of lost items. *He will see it,* she thought. *Leopard will see it, and there is no going back.* She tried to reassure herself. 'Of course you can go back,' she told herself. 'If you are frightened to go further, you can refuse to meet him.' But would she?

She called on the Jenningses, who were full of

excitement and flurry about the wedding preparations. 'I am sure I don't know why we are so flustered,' laughed Sophia. 'It is only a small wedding, and it is not as if we have time to do much.'

'But you are excited,' said Maisie, 'and that is natural.' She took in Sophia's sparkling eyes and flushed cheeks, and Inspector Hamilton came into her head quite unbidden, so that she had to bow her head and search for something in her bag rather hastily.

On her return to the hotel Maisie was surprised by the concierge hurrying over with a white envelope in his hand. 'A letter for you, Miss Frobisher,' he said. 'And if I'm not mistaken, that is the stationery of the civil service.'

'Thank you,' said Maisie, taking it and wishing that the concierge's powers of observation were slightly less acute. *Miss Frobisher, Hotel Victoria* was written in a bold black hand which, while dashing, retained a memory of letters carefully shaped under a master's observation. She smiled, and ripped it open.

Dear Miss Frobisher,

I hope you'll forgive me for wheedling your address out of the Darlings, but it was an emergency. Our men have returned successful from their expedition north, and old Howarth is so relieved that he's asked the governor to stand us a polo game and a spread later today. He said we could invite a guest, so I am inviting you. We shall be at the Mahalakshmi Race Ground at four o'clock.

Please say you'll come, it will be good fun.
Yours,

Edward Mandeville

'Good news, madame?' asked the concierge, still hovering.

'Yes,' said Maisie, 'very good news.' She transferred her smile from the note to him, then went to her room to consider her dresses and write a note of acceptance. *Really*, she thought, *things are moving very fast.* Was the pace of India always like this — periods of lassitude followed by a mad dash? 'I shall have to get used to it,' she said to herself, and pulled out her lilac dress for scrutiny.

At first Maisie had wondered whether the driver would know the way to the race ground; but when she gave the address he set off at such a clip that she arrived almost as breathless as if she had hurried there herself.

The players were already on their horses. Some walked them across to chat with the small group of spectators by the clubhouse, while others cantered, breaking into an occasional gallop, and swinging curious sticks rather like croquet mallets. A rider on a dark-brown horse spotted her and cantered over, lifting his hat. 'Miss Frobisher!' exclaimed Edward Mandeville. 'I hoped you would come.'

'I have never seen a game of polo before,' said Maisie. 'I am sure I shall enjoy it.'

'Sport of kings,' said Mr Mandeville. 'Isn't it, Marshall?'

Mr Marshall moved his horse round at the sound of his name. 'That it is,' he said, 'although I'm not sure how we shall make out.' He gaze shifted towards a distant figure on horseback. 'Howarth's playing.' Maisie followed his gaze to where Mr Howarth was exercising his horse in a most correct manner.

'Well, we must do the best we can,' said Mr Mandeville, resolutely. 'Play the game, and all that. There are drinks in the clubhouse, Miss Frobisher, if you'd like. Come on, Marshall, let's get these ponies warmed up.' And they rode off together.

Maisie watched them go, and noted how much more graceful Mr Mandeville looked on a horse than he did on his own two feet. *Or an elephant*, she added to herself, and chuckled.

'Now then, Miss Frobisher, what are you doing all alone?' Captain Hanson, as cool as ever, sauntered over. 'Why don't you come in and take a glass of something cold?'

'What a good idea,' said Maisie, and allowed herself to be led into the clubhouse, where a tall glass of lemonade was put in her hand. It was ice-cold, and very sharp.

'I think you know most people,' said the captain, and Maisie wondered if he was ever off duty as his eye roved around the company. 'I don't think you've met Miss Rose, so I shall introduce you.' He took Maisie's arm and escorted her across the room to where a willowy young lady in pale blue was speaking with Lady Montgomery and Mrs Smythe. 'Miss Rose, allow me to introduce Miss Frobisher, who is a new arrival in Bombay. Miss Frobisher, Miss Rose is the daughter of our Chief of Staff.' He nodded in satisfaction at having done his job, and withdrew.

'Delighted,' both ladies murmured.

'I did not expect to find you here, Miss Frobisher,' said Mrs Smythe, in a neutral tone.

'Mr Mandeville invited me,' said Maisie. 'I have never seen polo played before, and I'm sure it will be most instructive.'

'Of course it will not be like watching a proper polo match,' said Lady Montgomery. 'They are using their own horses, and naturally they will be careful of them. And also, I hope, of each other.' She laughed in a way that suggested she was a little disappointed that the game would not exhibit its usual ferocity.

'Is it usually violent?' asked Maisie.

'Oh no, I wouldn't say that,' Miss Rose assured her. 'But it is a fast game when played well, and sometimes the players cross each other's lines. You will see when it starts.'

'And speaking of starting,' said Lady Montgomery, 'aren't they supposed to be doing that at any moment? I shall go and let Geoffrey know. He does get very grumpy when he misses the beginning of things.' She looked around until she spotted the governor chatting to Mr Smythe, and headed towards him at a purposeful pace.

'I see you have adopted the uniform of the Raj,' said Miss Rose, gesturing at Maisie's dress. 'The Beaumonts must be rich enough to retire by now.' She laughed. 'It is much lighter to wear in this heat than our back-home dresses.'

'But possibly harder to take care of,' said Maisie. 'I pity my poor maid.'

'The Beaumonts are probably the worst-kept secret in

Bombay,' Miss Rose continued, as if Maisie's maid was not worth acknowledging. 'We do try to keep them to ourselves, but word always gets out somehow. Anyway, we had better get to the game.' She drank the last of her lemonade and strolled to the door.

Maisie glanced at Mrs Smythe, but her attention seemed to be elsewhere. She murmured 'Excuse me,' and followed Miss Rose.

The game had just begun, and Maisie scanned the field. From what she could tell one team wore blue sashes and the other red, and there appeared to be four players on each side. Another rider, not wearing a sash, cantered to and fro on his horse, following the game. 'He is the umpire,' said Miss Rose.

The game went back and forth, never reaching either end of the pitch. *The teams must be evenly matched*, thought Maisie. After a few minutes the umpire blew his whistle. 'That is the end of the first chukka,' said Miss Rose. 'They will get going again presently.'

'Who do you think will win?' asked Maisie, more for something to say than because she was particularly interested. She tried to pick out Edward Mandeville; but two players had dark-brown horses, which made identification difficult.

'Hard to say,' said Miss Rose, 'but I wouldn't bet against a side with Mr Howarth in it. He's very . . . diligent.' She shaded her eyes and peered down the field. 'Off they go.'

The game continued with more daring runs for goal, until eventually a horse broke free and galloped, its rider leaning to strike the ball with his mallet.

'It must take a lot of skill to learn how to ride and use a mallet at the same time,' said Maisie. 'I find it hard enough to play croquet on the ground.'

Miss Rose opened her eyes wide. 'It is a polo *stick*, dear, not a mallet.' And she turned back to the game. *It looks like a mallet to me,* thought Maisie.

Several chukkas later, and still apparently with no goals scored, the umpire blew a long blast on his whistle and the riders turned their horses towards the clubhouse. 'I could fancy another lemonade,' said Miss Rose. 'What an exciting game!' She eyed Maisie, and laughed. 'I don't think you found it as exciting as I did.'

'I might need a little more time to appreciate its subtleties,' said Maisie. 'But another drink does sound good.'

Little trays of sandwiches and pastries had been set out, and Maisie filled a modest plateful. She was about to bite into a cucumber sandwich when a hand touched her elbow and she found herself looking at the excited, flushed face of Edward Mandeville. 'What did you think? Did you enjoy it?' he cried.

She could not help smiling. 'Very much,' she said, 'although I must confess that I was not entirely sure what was going on.'

'You'll get the hang of it, Miss Frobisher,' he said heartily. 'Top game, though. I must say I was impressed with Mr Howarth.' His use of Mr Howarth's title conveyed that perhaps more than his tone. 'The chap can play, and no mistake. Have I got time for a sandwich, do you think?'

He dashed to the buffet and presently returned with a heaped plate, which he managed to work his way through while also discoursing on the iniquities of the right-hand side of the pitch, and his conviction that his stick was slightly shorter than those of the other players.

Mr Marshall joined them, and his laconic observations made a comical counterpoint to Edward Mandeville's enthusiastic outbursts. 'Now don't eat too much, Mandeville,' he said. 'You will give yourself indigestion, or possibly be too heavy for your poor horse.'

'Do be quiet, Marshall,' said Mr Mandeville; but he set his plate on a side table nevertheless.

The players departed to get ready for the second game, and Maisie caught sight of Miss Rose standing with Mrs Smythe in a corner. They appeared to be having a private conversation. *I won't disturb them*, she thought; but Miss Rose caught Maisie's eye, gave her such a malevolent look that Maisie almost recoiled, and then, very deliberately, turned her back on her.

Maisie went to get another glass of lemonade, her mind working furiously. Miss Rose had seemed friendly earlier, if a little contemptuous of Maisie's lack of polo knowledge. *What has happened to cause such a change in attitude?* Maisie glanced across again, and caught Mrs Smythe's satisfied smile. *You!* thought Maisie. *What have I ever done to you, except save your husband's job?* She sighed, sipped her lemonade, and walked outside.

The second game was more frenetic than the first, with more runs on the goals and more challenges as the players tried desperately to score before sunset stopped play.

Maisie stood in the shadow of the clubhouse, near enough to the other groups to seem unostracised. She might have joined a different group; but she did not wish to run the risk of another rejection.

At length one of the players in red sashes broke free, and as he charged she recognised Edward Mandeville making for the goal. Several other players were in hot pursuit. His face was set, determined, his eyes on the goal; but a player in a blue sash was chasing him down.

She heard the crack of a whip, and a horse bearing a red-sashed rider accelerated. She recognised Mr Howarth, standing in his stirrups and thrashing his horse. He passed the opposing player very close, caught up to Edward Mandeville, and leaning over, whacked the ball with his mallet. It skimmed the grass and rolled into the goal.

The red team cheered — except for Mr Mandeville, who looked disconsolate. Mr Howarth rode back and clapped him on the shoulder. 'I hope you don't mind, old man,' he said, 'but the goal was in danger, so I took action.'

'Of course not, sir,' said Edward Mandeville. 'What's best for the game, and all that.' But Maisie could see that it took an effort to keep the wavering smile on his face.

No more goals were scored, and victory was declared for the red team. Then they went to the clubhouse to eat and drink and review the game. Maisie kept at Edward Mandeville's side throughout. She couldn't risk Mrs Smythe turning him against her, as she had Miss Rose. *I don't understand*, she thought, as some of the players launched into a song which was apparently traditional at

Oxford after polo matches. *Why does she hate me so?* She did not dare to look for Mrs Smythe, to see where she was in the room, for she did not want to know where that lady would pour her poison next.

CHAPTER 9

Maisie woke before dawn the next day, and while the sight of the sunrise could have filled the most disappointed heart with awe and gratitude, Maisie remained unmoved. *You have come through worse*, she told herself. *At least you are not trapped on a ship with these people. You can leave on a boat or a train whenever you wish. Or shut yourself up in your room and wait until it blows over.* Her mind kept returning to the slights of the previous day, picking at them as one picks at a scab not ready to come off, and the nagging, sharp pain pulled at her constantly.

She was early to breakfast, in whatever dress came to hand; earlier even than the paper, which she requested specifically. 'Please bring one as soon as it arrives,' she said shortly, and the waiter looked rather affronted at her curt request.

Maisie drank cup after cup of coffee while she waited,

and ate pieces of a dry roll; she had no appetite for sweet things that morning. *Perhaps I should ask for a dish of bitter herbs as well*, she thought ruefully. *That, or a sour chutney.* She imagined Mrs Smythe making a breakfast of pickled cucumbers and unripe blackberries, and sniggered. 'If I had not given my word —' she muttered. But she had promised never to tell what had happened on board ship. *I do not know how I shall pay you back, Mrs Smythe*, she thought, ripping another piece from her roll and chewing hard, *but I shall*.

The newspaper came as Maisie was popping the last morsel of roll into her mouth. She nodded her thanks, and opened the paper as soon as the waiter had withdrawn. The personals column was on page nine, and she scanned the pages with an expert eye.

Nothing. No mention of Panther or Leopard, or indeed any other big cat. She reread the pages to make sure, closed the paper, and stalked to her room.

What now, Maisie thought, standing on her balcony and staring down at the garden. *Has our message scared Leopard off, or were we mistaken all this time?* She sighed and watched the scurrying servants below, busy with tasks that would probably be repeated the next morning, and the next.

What can I do? The thought of staying in her room all day was unappealing, and Maisie was in no mood to appreciate the sights of Bombay, however keen the concierge might be to supply information on them. She looked at her calling cards. She did not quite like to call on Mary Pike on a not-at-home day. She had called on Julia a few days before, and that call had not yet been returned. So that left Nora O'Connor. Maisie quailed at the thought of Nora's sly humour and sharp tongue; but perhaps her honesty would lead her to share what, if anything, she knew.

'Nora it is,' said Maisie, and began to make herself fit for a social call.

The O'Connors' bungalow was not as well situated as the Darlings', but still perfectly correct and presentable. Maisie sent in her card and waited. After three minutes she grew impatient, shifting from foot to foot. The day was beginning to warm up in earnest, and Maisie felt a bead of sweat trickling down her back. Was it her imagination, or could she hear raised voices? She retreated a few steps. If people were having an argument, or a heated discussion, she had no wish to hear it — and particularly not if it concerned her.

A few minutes later Nora herself, a little flushed, appeared at the door. 'Sorry to keep you waiting,' she said. 'Let's go to the summerhouse.' She stepped outside, walked quickly along the side of the house, and let herself into the garden through the little gate. Maisie noted that she did not offer an arm, or even look back.

The summerhouse was an octagonal wooden building, half an open deck with a rail and half enclosed. Nora opened the door and left it ajar, and when Maisie entered she found Nora already seated. 'It isn't really a summerhouse,' said Nora, 'since we were up in the hills and in Poona for summer, like everyone else —'

'Never mind that,' said Maisie. 'Tell me what's wrong.'

Nora picked at a fingernail. 'My mother was honoured by a call from Mrs Smythe yesterday,' she said. 'Once she had left, Mama summoned me and told me that I was to sever acquaintance with you.'

'What?' cried Maisie. 'Why?'

'I asked her exactly the same thing,' said Nora. 'Apparently Mrs Smythe had been given to understand that I was friendly with you. Mama refused to give me the particulars of what was said, but hinted that she had been told you were a fast young lady. "We can't have you tarred with the same brush, Nora," she said. "Imagine what it might do to your prospects."' Nora paused and looked speculatively at Maisie. 'If you don't mind me asking, what exactly *have* you done?'

How I wish I could tell you, thought Maisie, but realising that would not help matters, she left it unspoken. 'Nothing that I should be ashamed of,' she said firmly.

'I didn't think so,' said Nora. 'I told Mama how you blushed when we teased you about a certain young man, but she wasn't having any of it. Hence the commotion you heard just now. She said she wouldn't admit you under her roof, so I asked whether she would rather I took you to a cafe in the middle of Bombay, and apparently that wasn't right either. So we compromised on the summerhouse.' Then she frowned. 'What I don't understand is why Mrs Smythe would go to the trouble of calling. It isn't as if she's ever taken any notice of us before. I mean, we are invited to the parties, but I suspect that's more to do with Captain Hanson.' She looked rather pink herself at that point.

'If she's visited your mother, she's probably done the rounds of all my friends.' Maisie sighed. 'If it gets too bad I shall leave. I won't live in Bombay as a social outcast.'

'And you shouldn't have to,' said Nora heatedly. 'Not that I have any idea what you should do about it. Not unless you have friends in high places.'

Maisie opened her mouth to agree, then a thought struck her. One person definitely knew the truth of what had happened on the *SS Britannia*: the governor himself. And Inspector Hamilton would have the governor's ear. 'You are so clever!' she cried. She rose and hugged Nora. 'Now I shall leave before your mama comes to take you away from such a bad influence. Do give her my compliments.'

***

Maisie flagged down a rickshaw and gave directions for the Bombay Secretariat. The driver took her to an enormous building, built in the Venetian Gothic style, and she stared up at it in dismay before venturing into the foyer.

An Indian clerk was at the desk. 'Are you sure you are in the right place, ma'am?' he enquired primly.

'I think so,' said Maisie. 'Please could I borrow a pen and paper? I wish to leave a note for someone who works here.'

The clerk inclined his head, and passed her a sheet of paper, an envelope, and his fountain pen. Maisie thought for a minute, and wrote;

Dear Mr Hamilton,
Please could you favour me with a few minutes of your

time later today? I understand you are well-versed in law, and I would like to consult you on a small but pressing matter.

Yours sincerely,
Miss M Frobisher
P.S. I shall wait for an answer

She blew on the ink to dry it, sealed and addressed the envelope, and passed it to the clerk. 'Could you see that this is delivered quickly, please? I have said I shall wait for an answer.'

The clerk picked up what Maisie thought was a speaking tube, but instead of talking into it, he popped the note in and it vanished. 'It is delivered, madam,' he said. 'If you would like to take a seat over there…?'

Maisie obeyed and waited, fiddling with the clasp of her bag and watching the hands of the large clock on the opposite wall crawl their way round the dial. Five minutes later a muffled bell sounded. The clerk raised an eyebrow, unhooked the tube, and withdrew Maisie's envelope, now looking a little less crisp and fresh than when it had embarked on its journey. 'I take it you are Miss Frobisher,' he said, holding out the note.

'Indeed I am,' said Maisie, getting up and taking it from him. *Mr Hamilton* had been crossed out, and *Miss Frobisher* written in the inspector's spiky hand. *He has not adapted his writing to his new profession*, thought Maisie with a smile. The envelope had been hastily re-sealed with wax and an unfamiliar seal, not the crest which she would have expected. She broke it, and read:

Dear Miss Frobisher,

How pleasant to hear from you. I am pressed for time, but I could undertake to meet you for perhaps twenty minutes at lunchtime in order to discuss the matter you mention.

If you turn right out of this building there is a park two minutes' walk away. Please meet me at the third bench from the entrance at one o'clock, and we should be able to have a private conversation.

Yours sincerely,
F Hamilton, Esq

***

'This is rather irregular,' were the inspector's first words to Maisie as he sat down beside her, wearing a tweed suit which she suspected he would never have chosen of his own free will.

'I'm sorry,' said Maisie, 'but I must speak to you, and I didn't know what else to do.'

The inspector saw her expression, and his own softened. 'What is it?'

'Mrs Smythe is trying to poison the whole city against me,' said Maisie. 'Or at least, the female half. I went to a polo match yesterday, and a young woman who had been perfectly pleasant to me before cut me completely after a chat with Mrs Smythe. As well as that, she has paid calls on my friends' mothers to warn them about me.'

'I see,' said the inspector, his expression neutral.

'No you don't,' said Maisie. 'I don't expect you to understand, but you can help me to do something about it.'

'Can I?' He raised an eyebrow.

'Yes,' said Maisie. 'You can bring this to the attention of the governor, and get him to stop her.'

'I'm flattered that you think I have so much influence,' said Inspector Hamilton. 'What makes you think the governor will intervene?'

'Well, if you want me to meet this Leopard...' Maisie looked at him steadily. 'I assume I was invited to the governor's dinner for a reason. My hands are tied by my promise to keep quiet, but since the governor knows...'

'He may not wish to be reminded,' said Inspector Hamilton, with a wry twist of his mouth.

'Then perhaps he needs reminding,' said Maisie. 'He cannot expect me to help him, or you, if his own staff are getting in the way.'

'I take your point,' said the inspector. 'I shall wire the governor and request a meeting for both of us. I can't promise anything, but I shall do my best.'

'That's all I can ask of you,' said Maisie. 'I am very grateful.'

'I shall hope to see some demonstration of your gratitude at a more convenient time,' said the inspector, with a twinkle.

'Of course,' said Maisie. 'I shall send you a basket of fruit.' And with a twinkle of her own, she shook the inspector's hand.

***

Maisie returned to her hotel for lunch and then lay on her bed with a novel, resigned to a long wait. Yet the wait was not as long as she anticipated, for she was awakened by a tap at the door of her suite. Maisie padded to the door in stockinged feet, and opened it.

'Sorry to disturb you, madam, but I have a telegram,' said the attendant, handing it over. Maisie took the yellow envelope, gave him a coin, and gently closed the door.

Invited G House for 9 pm tonight. Will collect you at 8.30. FH

Maisie was wide-awake now, and despite the heat of the room, she felt as if she were the warmest thing in it by at least a hundred degrees. She had got her wish — a meeting with the governor — and now that she had it she was embarrassed by the thought of what she would have to say, and how it might be received. *But I must do it*, she thought, pressing her hands to her cheeks to cool them. *It is the only way I can continue to help, or indeed, to remain here.*

With that she bathed her face in cold water and made herself ready for afternoon tea. *I may be too nervous to eat later*, she thought, *and it will not do to faint in the presence of the governor.* That idea made her giggle, and she went down to the saloon feeling that if she could manage to laugh about it, it could not be so bad after all.

CHAPTER 10

'I don't understand,' said Ruth, as she fastened Maisie's necklace. 'What was the point of buying all those pretty dresses, if when you go to Government House you wear an old one?'

'I'm making a point,' said Maisie. 'If I had time I'd get a dress from the bazaar.'

Ruth tutted. 'It seems a waste to me, and I don't care who knows it. Especially when that nice Inspector Hamilton is taking you.'

'Oh, I don't doubt that he will be beautifully dressed,' said Maisie. 'He will relish the opportunity of wearing his best suit again. Off you go, for he is due soon.'

Ruth departed, still shaking her head, and Maisie sat down to wait for the inspector's arrival. How would he announce himself? She presumed that he would send a message — or would he attempt to scale her balcony? A broad smile lit up her face, and she opened the door to the balcony and peered out, heedless of the mosquitoes.

It was perhaps as well that she had; for the inspector was below and taking aim at her window. 'Ah, there you are,' he said, lowering his arm.

'Are you coming up?' asked Maisie, leaning on the rail.

'I hoped that you might come down,' he said. 'I don't think my suit will be improved by climbing.'

'I shall leave the hotel in the usual manner,' said Maisie firmly.

'What a shame,' said the inspector. 'I was looking forward to watching you attempt the descent.' He grinned. 'Our carriage is waiting, and I shall probably be in it by the time you emerge.' He tipped his hat, and strolled off.

Maisie pinned on her hat, caught up her gloves and bag, and locked the door feeling rather apprehensive. Would her choice of outfit be seen as flippant, or rude even? Well, arriving late would probably be even worse.

A closed carriage was waiting outside the hotel. As Maisie approached the door opened and she saw that Inspector Hamilton was within. 'Good evening, madam,' he said. 'What a beautiful night for a drive.' Something in his tone reassured Maisie, and once the doorman had handed her in, she leaned back against the cushions. The inspector knocked on the panel, and they moved off.

Inspector Hamilton was, as she had surmised, wearing the suit she knew from the cruise ship; but the moonlight showed a line of worry between his eyebrows which she longed to smooth away. He caught her look and smiled, then his gaze took in her dress. 'What, no muslin?' he said.

'No,' said Maisie. 'There seems little point in wearing out my new wardrobe when people are actively working to discredit me. Not all the muslin in the world can change that.'

'I take your point,' said the inspector. 'Lord Montgomery may not, though.'

Maisie shrugged. 'He may think what he pleases,' she said, and looked out of the window.

She felt a light touch on her arm, and stiffened. 'I will support you,' said the inspector, 'but I'm warning you that it may not be easy. No doubt the governor has his own agenda. I daresay he would not have granted an audience if he wanted nothing from us.'

Maisie sighed. 'I appreciate what you are doing, really I do. It just seems so —'

'Silly?' He smiled at her expression. 'I agree. Yet it is worth bringing to the governor's attention, not only because of the distress it is causing you, but for its own sake. I would raise the matter even if I didn't think that more than one woman's fear and jealousy lay behind it. Now prepare yourself, for we are at Government House.'

The carriage turned in at the driveway and headed for the steps; yet it did not stop, but continued round the side of the house and further into the grounds.

'What's going on?' cried Maisie, gripping the inspector's hand. 'Where is he taking us?'

The inspector winced and gently disengaged himself. 'Following orders.'

The carriage drew to a halt outside a small wooden gate. Inspector Hamilton opened the carriage door and helped Maisie out, then held the gate open for her. He took her arm and led her into the garden, down a dusty path, and not far away Maisie saw the summerhouse they had sat in briefly during the governor's reception. That seemed years ago. The inspector opened the door, and they entered.

The summerhouse was lit with candles in glass holders, which gave an eerie, flickering light. A tray stood ready with a pot of peppermint tea and glasses, and a covered dish held biscuits.

'See,' said the inspector, placing a chair for Maisie. 'We are expected.'

Expected they might be; but nine o'clock came and went with no sign of a governor or anyone connected to him.

Maisie fidgeted and helped herself to another biscuit. 'He will come, won't he?'

'I assume so,' said Inspector Hamilton. 'He is probably detained by business.'

It was fully twenty past nine before the door opened and Lord Montgomery entered, pipe in hand. 'Dinner guest,' he said, sitting down. 'Couldn't get him to leave. One of those professional travellers who have letters of introduction to take them around the globe.' He looked disgusted. 'I told Rowena I was going for a smoke to get the taste of him out of my mouth. That gives us half an hour.'

Maisie felt warning pressure against her right foot, and closed her mouth.

'Thank you for seeing us at such short notice, Lord

Montgomery,' said Inspector Hamilton.

'It's easy when it doesn't have to be a dinner or reception,' said the governor. 'Damn Hanson books them full of young 'uns wanting a good time. I feel like a rich uncle.' He sighed. 'Anyway, Hamilton, what was it you wanted so urgently?'

'It's more to do with Miss Frobisher,' said the inspector. 'Your new Secretary's wife is trying to ruin her reputation.'

'Is she, indeed,' said Lord Montgomery, sticking his pipe in his mouth and rummaging for a match.

'Yes, she is,' said Maisie. 'A friend of mine hinted at what has been happening, and a new acquaintance cut me completely at the polo match yesterday, after Mrs Smythe spoke to her.'

The governor looked at her keenly. 'Do you mind if I smoke?' he asked.

'Of course not,' said Maisie, aggrieved that Lord Montgomery's pipe seemed more important to him than her reputation. 'But I do mind her behaviour, and I want her to stop it.'

'I see.' Lord Montgomery struck a match on the sole of his shoe and applied it to his pipe, puffing until it was well established. 'What if I said that, while I do not condone her behaviour, it has proved rather useful?'

'What?!' cried Maisie, and stood up. The inspector stood too, and tried to take Maisie's arm, but she shook him off. 'How can *that* be useful?'

'Well, now,' said Lord Montgomery, with a twinkle in his eye. 'Since Hamilton here let me know about this

Leopard who has been advertising in the *Bombay Telegraph*, I asked the fellows at the newspaper to send me advance warning of any messages for the personal column which might be connected. I received a wire earlier which may interest you.' He paused. 'If you don't mind sitting down, Miss Frobisher.'

Maisie sat, slowly, and the governor fished in the inner pocket of his tailcoat. 'Here we are.' He put on a pair of spectacles, unfolded the telegram, and read: 'My dear Panther, how lovely to make your acquaintance. We must meet; but Bombay is no place for big cats to play. Leopard.' He took off his spectacles and studied Maisie. 'What do you make of that, Miss Frobisher?'

'He wants us to meet elsewhere,' Maisie replied, and she shivered despite the heat.

'Exactly,' said the governor. 'It would make sense for a young lady under a cloud to go away for a bit, wouldn't it?'

'It would,' said Maisie. 'I can't say I like it, though.'

'I don't suppose you do,' said Lord Montgomery. 'But there it is.' He turned to the inspector. 'Now, Hamilton, do you have anything new to tell me?'

'I'm glad you think it's settled, Lord Montgomery,' said Maisie, standing up. 'I owe no obligation to you, and I want no further part in this. I shall take the next boat back to England.'

She made for the door; but as she turned the handle the governor spoke again. 'Miss Frobisher, I beg you to reconsider. You are the only person who can perform this service for me.'

Maisie turned and regarded him. 'So what will you do

for me in return, Lord Montgomery?'

'While you are away I shall speak to the Smythes, and make it clear that Mr Smythe's position as Secretary is dependent on his wife retracting whatever false statements she has made, and apologising to you in public on your return.' He raised an eyebrow. 'Will that do?'

'What if I don't return?' said Maisie. When the words had left her mouth she realised what she had said, and gasped in horror.

'It's a distinct possibility,' the governor admitted.

'No it isn't,' said Inspector Hamilton. He walked over to Maisie and took her hand. 'Whatever it is, wherever it is, I'm going with you.'

'That depends, surely,' said the governor.

'No it doesn't,' said the inspector. 'It's both of us, or neither.'

The governor eyed them both, then laughed softly. 'So that's how it is,' he said. 'Very well. Once we know where Miss Frobisher is heading, I shall do my best to get you there on official business.'

'Thank you, Lord Montgomery,' said Inspector Hamilton.

The governor blew a smoke ring. 'I thought you would make that condition. Not because there is anything between you, of course —' His eyes gleamed in the low light. 'You have grown accustomed to working together. Since you seem keen to take your leave, I shall let you go and enjoy my pipe. Wire when you know more.' And with that he sat back in his chair, stuck his legs out, and closed his eyes.

Maisie's hand found the inspector's as they walked down the dark path. 'Don't worry,' he said, squeezing it.

'But I do worry,' said Maisie. 'He was so calm when I said I might not come back. He doesn't care about me at all.'

The inspector continued to press her hand, but said no more until they were in the carriage and heading into Bombay. 'Look at it from his point of view,' he said. 'Lord Montgomery doesn't know *you*. But he does know that you have managed, with me, to prevent the theft of an important and confidential document. The latest information leak to the maharajah, if he had not been placated, could have caused an uprising, and potentially several deaths. If that were escalated...' Even in the dim light Maisie could see how serious his face was. 'The last thing India needs is another mutiny.'

'Do you think that might happen?' asked Maisie, tremulously.

'I hope not,' said Inspector Hamilton. 'I hope both sides would be able to compromise, and settle their differences with words rather than bayonets and guns. But someone clearly wants to stir up as much trouble as they can. In these temperatures it does not take a great deal for tempers to flare.' He focused on Maisie. 'Set against that, the life of one person probably doesn't weigh so heavy in the balance.'

'I see,' said Maisie, blinking furiously.

'Whereas I, of course, think you are extremely important.' His hand reached for hers.

'Oh, do stop it,' Maisie choked out, squeezing the

inspector's hand so hard that she heard a sharp intake of breath.

'I do wish you'd make your mind up,' he said. 'First you are cross that I don't take enough notice of you, and when I do say something nice you tell me to be quiet.'

'I'm not used to it,' said Maisie. 'Perhaps you should do it more often, and then it would be less of a shock.'

'Perhaps I should,' said the inspector, and she could hear the smile in his voice. 'Particularly when we are in a closed carriage in the dark, and all alone…' He leaned closer, until she could feel his warm breath on her face —

'Victoria Hotel, sir!' cried the driver, and the carriage slowed.

'I don't believe it,' muttered the inspector. 'If I were superstitious I would say that I was under some sort of curse.' He sat back and adjusted his bow tie. 'If anything happens wire me at the office, or send in a note. That's safest.'

'I shall,' said Maisie automatically, for her mind was on very different matters. 'I'm sorry about your tie.'

The inspector looked down. 'What about my —'

Maisie leaned forward and pulled his tie undone. Holding the ends, she drew him towards her and kissed him. 'For doing that,' she said softly, and released him. 'Will you hand me out of the carriage, please?'

The inspector was silent, and Maisie was rather glad that the carriage was too dark to see his expression. 'No, I shan't,' he replied curtly, then rapped on the panel. 'Driver! Take us to the Hanging Gardens and back, please. Not too fast.'

'Yes, sir,' said the driver, and they set off again at a slow pace.

'That gives us roughly ten minutes,' said Inspector Hamilton. 'That's as much time as I can spend alone with you without compromising us both beyond repair, but a fraction of the time I want. Now, where were we?' And as he leaned towards her Maisie thought that perhaps the risk of death was a small price to pay.

CHAPTER 11

It was a small congregation. No more than three rows in the little church; and many of those people were friends of Mrs Ponsonby, whom she had invited to 'make up the numbers', as she put it. The Smythes had given their apologies, pleading an important work engagement. Nevertheless, Sophia and her fiancé glowed with pride and happiness. Mr Ponsonby had given Sophia away, and very beautiful she looked as she walked down the aisle in her floaty white dress. Christopher Merritt had had a new suit made for the occasion, Mrs Ponsonby's granddaughter was a flower girl, and all in all everything was most correct. Some people had commented on the lack of bridesmaids; but then the couple had just arrived in India.

Sophia had asked Maisie privately if she could be her bridesmaid, but on discovering that she would be the only one Maisie had declined. 'I should feel so odd,' she said,

'And besides, I have known you a very short while, comparatively speaking.'

Sophia sighed. 'I suppose,' she said, and left it at that.

Maisie had felt guilty for disappointing her friend; but now she was glad that she had refused. She had taken the precaution of sitting at the far end of a pew, next to the Fortescues, but even so she sensed people looking at her, and heard the occasional whisper about 'that Miss Frobisher'.

It had been a strange, lonely week. Sophia had hinted that she might bring a guest if she wished; and so she had sent a tentative invitation to Mr Mandeville. In reply she had received a short note.

Dear Miss Frobisher,
Unfortunately I have already made plans for this weekend, and therefore I cannot accept your kind invitation.
Yours sincerely,
E. Mandeville

Maisie tried not to read too much into it; but that 'E', the withholding of his first name, spoke volumes. And while the Darlings had said in private that of course they didn't believe the rumours, they also said that perhaps it would be best not to be seen together until the whole matter blew over. 'People talk, you see,' said Julia Darling. 'And while we do support you, Maisie, some of our less understanding friends would ostracise us if they saw us with you. I know the Roses are planning a ball, and if

Ethel thinks that we are friendly with you she will excommunicate us. If we were shunned by the Chief of Staff's daughter, we would be cast into the outer darkness.' She laughed a brittle laugh which Maisie presumed was meant to convey that such things did not matter to her; but clearly they did.

The priest's voice rose, and Maisie shook herself from her unpleasant thoughts and paid attention. 'I pronounce that they be man and wife together, in the Name of the Father, and of the Son, and of the Holy Ghost. Amen.' He paused. 'You *may* kiss the bride,' he hinted to Mr Merritt, who obeyed, his face flushed pink, and the congregation broke out in laughter and applause, almost drowning the priest's blessing.

The new Mr and Mrs Merritt posed on the steps of the church for a photograph, which took an inordinate length of time; for the photographer kept adjusting his tripod, disappearing under his black cloth, then reappearing to declare that the light was all wrong. Eventually, though, it was done, and the party repaired to Mrs Ponsonby's house, where a dainty wedding breakfast awaited them on the veranda.

Maisie nibbled at a canapé and chatted with the mother of the bride, who was very smart in her new half-mourning and more voluble than Maisie had ever known her. 'Didn't it go well, Miss Frobisher?' said Mrs Jennings, reaching for a biscuit. 'I couldn't sleep last night for worrying, and I couldn't eat a morsel this morning. I'm so relieved it's over. Don't they make a handsome pair?'

'Oh, they do,' said Maisie. Sophia and Christopher

were talking with Inspector Hamilton. Now that the deed was done Christopher Merritt seemed to have lost his awkwardness, and Sophia looked beautiful in her simple white dress. Maisie's gaze shifted to the inspector, who was smiling and chatting easily, a glass of lemonade in his hand. Maisie could scarcely believe that he was the same man who had kissed her in the carriage only a few evenings before. Then Inspector Hamilton caught her looking, and casually fiddled with the knot of his tie. Maisie gasped, and the corner of his mouth quirked up in a way which made her quiver.

'We haven't seen much of Inspector Hamilton lately,' said Mrs Jennings thoughtfully. 'He must be working hard, although I'm sure I don't know what he's doing. Really, I've been so busy with the wedding that I have barely taken notice of anything else. Have *you* been doing anything interesting, my dear?' She turned a polite smile on Maisie, who blessed her preoccupation.

'Nothing of note,' she replied. 'It is too hot to do anything. I plan to visit Calcutta for a change, since I hear it is cooler on the other coast.'

'Oh, you are travelling again?' said Mrs Jennings. 'Sophia and — her husband will be going away after the wedding breakfast. His company has use of a lodge up in the hills, at Mahabaleshwar, and they have made him a present of it for a few days.'

'How delightful,' said Maisie.

Her train ticket had arrived two days ago, in an envelope printed with her name. The enclosed note said: *Travel light. From a friend.* The ticket was for the Indian

Mail, leaving Bombay for Calcutta at noon on Saturday.

Maisie had wired Inspector Hamilton and the governor immediately, and both had responded by return. That evening they had met in the summerhouse again; and this time Lord Montgomery had been punctual. Neither had he smoked. 'I have presents,' he said, reaching into the pocket of his linen jacket. 'For you, Inspector, a train ticket and a commission.' He handed Inspector Hamilton an envelope. 'The viceroy has planned to undertake survey work west of Calcutta for some time, and I informed him today by letter that I have just the man for the job. I also wired to inform him of the letter, including a code word to alert him that you are a person of interest. He wired by return that he was officiating at a reception on Monday evening, and that you may introduce yourself there.' He paused. 'Since we don't know what this Leopard is planning, it is as well for you to have a reason for your presence in Calcutta. I shall inform Howarth of your new role tomorrow.' He fumbled in his pocket again. 'Miss Frobisher, I have something for you to look after.' He handed her a small packet of folded oilcloth.

Maisie stared at it. 'Do I open it?'

The governor let out a laugh which was almost a bark. 'Of course you open it!'

Carefully Maisie unwrapped the package. Inside was a piece of folded parchment which seemed horribly familiar. She unfolded it and gasped as her suspicions were confirmed.

'It is a very good copy,' said the governor. 'Rewritten to be considerably less agitating if it did get into the wrong hands — which it well may do. If it does I am perfectly willing to disown it as an obvious forgery; but to a casual eye, it will pass.' He turned to the inspector. 'I take it you have a gun?'

'Of course,' said Inspector Hamilton.

'And what about you, Miss Frobisher?'

'Me?' said Maisie. 'I — I never thought —'

'I suspected you might not have.' The governor got up, and pressed down on a floorboard with his heel. The other end of the board rose, he slid it out, and revealed a little box which he put on the table. He opened it to reveal a small pearl-handled gun and a box of bullets. 'This is ready to use except for loading,' he said, 'which I shall do now. I hope you won't have to use it, but keep it about your person. If anyone asks, you have it because you are frightened of being robbed. It isn't the most accurate weapon, but it will do at a pinch.' He took off the safety catch, aimed the pistol at the door, and pointed at the trigger. 'I'm sure you can take it from there.' He lowered the gun, put the safety catch back on, and replaced it in the box. 'I had better go before I am missed; Hanson is bound to want me to say goodbye to somebody. But I shall say goodbye to you first, and wish you the best of luck. I hope to see you both again soon.' He shook their hands very firmly, then opened the door, stuck his hands in his pockets, and went out whistling.

***

'Maisie, come quickly!'

Maisie blinked and looked into Sophia's smiling, puzzled face. 'You were miles away. Hurry, I am about to throw the bouquet!'

Maisie followed her friend onto the lawn. All the unmarried ladies were gathered in a huddle, while everyone else stood apart, laughing and joking. Maisie took up a position on the edge, while Sophia dashed forward and stood with her back to them. 'One, two, three!' she cried, and threw the bouquet over her head.

It arced high in the air, and seemed set to land in the middle of the group. A hand shot up to catch it, but knocked it sideways. The bouquet touched Maisie's raised right hand, and instinctively her fingers closed round it.

'Ow!' she cried, and nearly dropped it, for she had grasped a thorn. Maisie transferred the flowers to her other hand and grinned as broadly as she could.

'You're next, Maisie!' called Sophia, beaming.

There were a few stiff murmurs of 'well done' from the other ladies, coupled with whispers, and a general consensus that dear Sophia hadn't thrown well at all. Maisie didn't dare to look at Inspector Hamilton for some time; but when she did his eyes were on her, and he smiled a slow smile. *I am going on a train journey with that man*, she thought, and her heart pounded.

'Well done, my dear,' said Mrs Fortescue, bustling up and kissing her cheek. 'Don't you worry about those cats. And on that note we must say goodbye, for the colonel and I are going north this afternoon, and I'm sure there is something I have forgotten to pack.' The colonel ambled over too and shook hands all round, before the pair descended on the happy couple.

The Merritts' carriage arrived to bear them off on

honeymoon, and in the general fluster of loading their luggage and saying their farewells it was easy for Maisie to slip away. She could have stayed a little longer; but she wanted to leave with happy thoughts of the Merritts in her mind. And as her rickshaw lurched through the streets of Bombay, Maisie wondered if she would ever see them again.

CHAPTER 12

Ruth folded Maisie's underthings with her usual care and laid them on top of her spare dress. Then she slammed the lid of the suitcase and fastened the clasps. 'I know you could have taken me, Miss Frobisher,' she said. 'I made enquiries.'

'I don't have a ticket for you, Ruth,' said Maisie. 'In any case, I do not plan to be away for long. I should return within the week.'

'So you aren't sure.' Ruth drew herself up to her full height and glared at Maisie. 'What's going on?'

'I am travelling to Calcutta by train,' Maisie replied, lifting her chin so that she could look Ruth in the eye. 'That is all you need to know, Ruth. I can always wire the hotel if I require your services.'

'So I am to stay here and twiddle my thumbs till you get back?' Ruth was so overcome that she sat on the bed.

'What will I do with myself?' She put her head in her hands and her shoulders shook.

'Oh, Ruth...' Maisie sat down beside her and put an arm round her shoulders.

'I just wish you'd tell me!' Ruth wailed. 'I may be only your maid, but —'

'I can't, Ruth. I simply can't.' Maisie opened the drawer of her bureau and took out a sealed envelope. 'I shall be in touch as soon as I can. If I haven't wired by this time next week...' She put the envelope in Ruth's hands. 'Then, you open this.' Following much thought the previous evening, she had written a letter to each of her parents and a note to Ruth, in which she had enclosed enough money for Ruth's passage home.

Ruth stared at the envelope, then bundled it into her petticoat pocket. 'I don't want to know what it says.' She bounced up and folded Maisie in an angular hug. 'Just you be careful, Miss Maisie. I don't know what scrape you're getting yourself into this time, but be careful.'

'I shall,' said Maisie, returning the hug.

A tap at the door announced the porter. 'The carriage is waiting, ma'am,' he said, and picked up Maisie's cases.

Ruth burst into sobs, and after an awkward pat or two Maisie whispered 'Goodbye for now,' kissed her damp cheek, and closed the door gently behind her.

***

'Boarding for Calcutta!' The guard, resplendent in epaulettes and brass buttons not so dissimilar from Captain Carstairs's uniform, marched along the platform, shouting his refrain between blasts of his whistle. A porter rushed to

Maisie's carriage, helped her down, and set about her suitcases. 'I'll take this to the luggage van, madam,' he said, picking up the larger of the two.

'Thank you,' said Maisie, giving him a coin. He pocketed it and lifted his cap. 'Much obliged, madam. Do you know which carriage you are in?'

Maisie opened her bag and consulted her ticket. 'This says cabin thirteen.'

'Oho!' cried the porter. 'Then you are almost at the end of the train.' He pointed to Maisie's overnight case, which was sizeable. 'Shall I call another porter, madam?'

'I can help the lady with that,' said a familiar voice. Maisie turned to see Inspector Hamilton, dressed for travelling in a linen suit and Panama hat and carrying a small case. He lifted her suitcase as if it were empty. 'Shall we?'

They walked down the platform in silence for a few moments, dodging porters and piles of luggage and tearful farewells. 'Travelling light, eh?' The inspector smiled.

'This *is* light,' said Maisie. 'You should have seen the trunk I brought with me on the ship.'

'Oh, I did,' said the inspector, with feeling.

'Anyway,' said Maisie, 'how did the office take your departure?'

'With equanimity, mostly,' Inspector Hamilton replied. 'I suspect most of them are glad to see the back of me. Howarth isn't happy, though. Apparently he's well overdue a trip to Calcutta, but the governor never lets him leave the secretariat; he's too indispensable. Marshall told me on the quiet that Howarth's desperate to get within touching distance of the Viceroy.'

'That's a pity,' said Maisie, looking at the enormous train before them, a vision of gold and green paint, belching smoke and huffing to be gone. Despite herself, she couldn't help being excited at the thought of a journey across India.

'It is, rather,' said the inspector. He leaned closer, and murmured in her ear. 'Especially when you think of someone like Smythe, who has travelled the world doing precisely nothing.'

'Which is your cabin?' asked Maisie.

Inspector Hamilton raised an eyebrow. 'Should I really tell you that?' He grinned. 'In case you need to know, I am in cabin ten.'

An official glanced up, then rushed over, arm raised. 'Sir, sir! There has been a change.'

The inspector stopped dead. 'What sort of change?'

'A change of cabin,' the official said, panting. 'See, it is on my list. A last-minute booking, and as he is a colleague of yours —'

'Ah, there you are, Hamilton.' Mr Howarth bore down on them, a battered portmanteau in his hand. 'Sorry to surprise you. I had a chat with the governor, you see, and he is a little worried about you taking this job on solo, so I volunteered to ride shotgun, so to speak.' He beamed at the inspector, and then his eye fell on Maisie. 'Good afternoon, Miss Frobisher. I didn't realise that you two knew each other.'

'Mr Hamilton was helping with my luggage,' said Maisie. 'We have met a few times at Government House.'

'Oh yes, of course.' Mr Howarth transferred his attention back to the inspector. 'We are somewhere in the middle…'

'Cabin five,' the official interjected.

'That's it.' Mr Howarth clapped his colleague on the back. 'Come and join me when you've finished with Miss Frobisher's bags.' And off he went.

'Damn,' said the inspector, under his breath. 'What a time for Howarth to pull rank.'

'The very worst,' said Maisie. 'You don't think…?'

'For all I know the governor's sent him to keep an eye on me,' said Inspector Hamilton. 'Maybe he doesn't trust me, either.' He sighed. 'Come on, or the train will leave without us.' And the official tapped his watch significantly.

The inspector struggled manfully down the narrow corridor with Maisie's overnight and dressing cases. 'They ought to have luggage restrictions,' he grumbled. Maisie said nothing, sensing that his ill-humour was directed at Mr Howarth and the governor rather than herself. The door to cabin thirteen was open. Inspector Hamilton walked in and set the cases down, then touched his hat.

'Thank you,' said Maisie. 'Perhaps I shall see you in the dining car.'

'Perhaps,' said the inspector. 'No tip, m'lady?'

Maisie glanced along the corridor, where a uniformed shape was moving in their direction. 'Not on this occasion,' she said, smiling. 'I'll have to save it for later.'

The official who had redirected the inspector hurried towards them. 'There you are, sir,' he said reproachfully. He took a large ring of keys from his pocket, peered at it, then worked a key off the ring and handed it to Maisie. 'Please take great care of this, madam. Only the guard has a spare one, since yours is a single cabin.' He replaced the ring of keys in his pocket and checked his large fob watch. 'We shall depart in five minutes. Luncheon will be served at one o'clock in the dining car, and this afternoon I shall visit you and demonstrate the fixtures and fittings of your cabin.'

'Thank you so much,' said Maisie, trying not to laugh.

'It is my pleasure, madam,' he replied, with a jerky little bow like a mechanical toy. 'Now, sir, I shall show you to your cabin and give you your key. Good afternoon, madam.' And he closed the door smartly behind himself and the inspector, with the air of a man who has done his job entirely to his own satisfaction.

Maisie surveyed her cabin. A seat which pulled down from the wall, and a flat surface which swung on a hinge and latched into place; a bed which presumably folded out, and a little washstand in the corner. 'It will certainly do for two days,' she said aloud. 'I imagine there is a saloon somewhere, as well as the dining car.' The guard's whistle blew a long blast, and the train hooted in reply.

Maisie felt a jolt, and looked out of the window. The train was already moving, and those left on the platform glided past, waving and blowing kisses. If only she had someone to wave to; her parents, or dear Connie, or Sophia, or even Ruth. Maisie bit her lip and waved anyway, hoping that someone, somewhere, was wishing her safe travels.

CHAPTER 13

It was five minutes to one when Maisie began to hear doors opening, and the hum of low voices as people passed. *Just like the Britannia,* she thought. *Except that presumably we choose our own tables.* She checked her reflection in the glass, wished that Ruth was there to tidy her hair, picked up her bag, and sallied forth.

The dining and saloon car was situated towards the rear of the train; a mahogany sign announced it with gold letters and a pointing hand. Maisie walked slowly, trying to balance herself with the swaying motion of the train, as trees swept by outside the window. Ahead she could see the backs of her fellow passengers; Panama hats and caps and straw hats and day dresses. What would they be like?

A waiter welcomed her at the door of the dining room. 'I hope madam will not mind sharing a table,' he said, nervously, 'but as madam is alone —'

'Oh no, that's quite all right,' said Maisie.

'Very good, madam,' he said approvingly. 'If you would come this way?'

Maisie glanced at each table as she passed, trying to see the inspector, and, she supposed, Mr Howarth. If she could claim acquaintance with them there was a chance of communicating with the inspector. But the waiter hurried to the back of the dining room. 'I have a very good seat for you, madam,' he said. 'I shall put you with Mr Ainsley and Mr and Mrs Carter. Yes. Here we are.'

He indicated with a flourish a table unoccupied save for a raised newspaper. 'Good afternoon, Mr Ainsley,' said the waiter brightly. 'I am sure that you will not mind sharing a table with Miss Frobisher.'

The newspaper lowered, and a pair of beady black eyes looked into Maisie's. 'Of course not,' said Mr Ainsley, folding the paper. He was elderly, with sallow skin which reminded Maisie of parchment. 'Good afternoon, Miss Frobisher.' He said the words with old-world courtesy; but Maisie felt as if those birdlike eyes saw everything.

'I shall bring your menus when everyone is seated.' The waiter bowed, and trotted away to deal with the next arrivals.

'So,' said Mr Ainsley, 'what takes you to Calcutta, Miss Frobisher? I assume you *are* going all the way to Calcutta, and not getting off somewhere in the interior.'

'Oh, just travelling,' said Maisie. 'I have seen something of Bombay, and Calcutta seemed like the next place to go.' She laughed in what she hoped was a suitably frivolous manner.

'Oh yes, travelling,' said Mr Ainsley. 'Some people travel to escape, don't they? I am glad that you are not one of those, Miss Frobisher. We can never escape from ourselves, can we?'

Maisie opened her mouth and closed it again, uncertain of what she could say to such a remark. She drank from her glass of water instead, and was glad when the waiter came bustling up, escorting two more passengers. 'Mr and Mrs Carter, may I introduce Mr Ainsley and Miss Frobisher. I shall go and get your menus.' And he sprang off, Maisie thought, rather as one of the frog footmen in *Alice in Wonderland* might do.

Mrs Carter sat in the seat next to Maisie, and her husband sat opposite. They were perhaps in their forties, and while Mr Carter was lean and tanned, Mrs Carter was plump and pink-faced. 'Such a rush,' she said, shaking out a napkin. 'I wish they would change the start time of the trains. One barely has time to get on and get oneself organised before lunch — and what a lunch — and then the steward will come along afterwards and insist on showing one which way the handles turn, and what all the buttons do.'

'I take it you have travelled on this train before,' said Maisie, smiling.

Mrs Carter heaved a theatrical sigh. 'My dear, I swear that there have been times when I felt like nothing more than an enormous bandalore, travelling back and forth, back and forth on the railway, accompanying Randolph on his assignments.'

'It really wasn't that bad, Estella,' said Mr Carter

mildly.

The waiter reappeared with their menus and Maisie bent her head to study hers, reflecting that while Mr Carter could be imagined as a Randolph, she would never have placed Mrs Carter as an Estella. 'Good heavens,' she murmured, as she read.

'I *know*,' said Mrs Carter, laying a hand on her forearm. 'At least we don't have to eat all of it.'

Maisie's eyes travelled down the list of options, rejecting most of them at a glance. 'I shall have the sole meunière followed by lime sorbet,' she said firmly. 'That is quite enough lunch for me.'

'Are you following a diet, Miss Frobisher?' Mrs Carter asked earnestly. 'Perhaps I ought to, for I do suffer from indigestion, but I think it is the climate. I never used to suffer at home.'

'How long have you been in India, Mrs Carter?' Maisie asked.

'Twenty-one years,' said Mrs Carter briskly. 'Except when I was taking the darling children back to live with dear Mama. They are at boarding school now, so we are well settled.' Maisie thought of Edward Mandeville, and wondered whether his family were anything like the Carters. 'I think I shall have the steak,' Mrs Carter continued. 'They do cook it excellently, and I must admit it is rather a treat, for as many of our servants are Hindus I would never dare to ask for it at home.' Mrs Carter beamed with anticipation, and Maisie could not help smiling. *After all*, she reflected, *if I could eat beef perhaps once every six months, I should look forward to a steak too.*

The waiter returned, and the party gave their orders. Maisie noticed that while Mr Ainsley asked for a small bottle of wine, he ordered only a Welsh rarebit and extra toast to go with it. 'One's digestion is not what it was,' he said grudgingly. 'Too many chilies.'

'Have you travelled much in India, Mr Ainsley?' asked Maisie.

'Not particularly,' he said drily. 'I have sold up and retired, but until recently I was a merchant — a boxwallah, if you like. I have attended more shooting parties as a guest of my clients than I care to think of. At those, the food is very spicy.'

'A big-game hunter, eh?' said Mr Carter.

'I am no great shot,' said Mr Ainsley laconically. 'But I have seen more tigers and leopards taken down than Miss Frobisher has had hot dinners, I daresay.' His beady black eyes settled on Maisie's face, and she fought the urge to turn away.

They made small talk until the waiter brought their food. Maisie's sole was excellent. 'I don't know how they do it,' she said, as she put her knife and fork down on the almost-bare plate.

'Practice,' said Mr Carter. 'If you have to cook for thirty demanding passengers three times a day, you will soon become good at it.'

Maisie laughed. 'I'm not sure my friends' cooks have had such training,' she said.

The sorbet was equally good; tart and refreshing with just the right amount of sweetness. Maisie sighed with pleasure. 'I wish I could give my cook the recipe for that,' she said.

'It did look very nice,' said Mrs Carter, who was engaged with a charlotte russe. 'I had forgotten how large these are. I may need a little nap after lunch.'

'If you will choose a heavy pudding...' her husband chided gently. 'I shall go for a smoke once we have finished. Mr Ainsley, would you care to join me?'

'By all means,' said Mr Ainsley, pulling his pipe and tobacco pouch from his pocket.

The dessert dishes were cleared, and coffee was served with little shortbread biscuits. Maisie sipped hers, but it was very strong; so strong that she felt her pulse quicken in response. She put down her cup, and when she glanced up found Mr Ainsley studying her. He didn't look away, but continued to tamp the tobacco in his pipe with an amused expression.

Maisie poured herself another glass of water. Her mouth was dry as a bone. *Why is he staring at me like that?* And then she recalled his remark about shooting tigers and leopards. Had it been a coincidence?

Is Mr Ainsley Leopard?

She took another gulp of water. 'If you would excuse me, I might take a nap too,' she said. 'That sorbet was so delicious that I ate it too quickly, and it has brought on a headache.'

'Oh, you poor dear,' said Mrs Carter. 'Do you need anything? Smelling salts, or eau de cologne?'

'No, no,' Maisie said hastily, for Mrs Carter was already opening her capacious handbag. 'I'm sure a nap will put me right.' She rose, managed a weak smile, and walked carefully down the dining car to the exit. Now she could see Mr Howarth and the inspector, of course; but Inspector Hamilton was facing away from her, and being lectured by Mr Howarth about rods and poles.

The waiter hurried towards her with a concerned expression on his face. 'Is everything all right, madam?'

'Oh yes,' said Maisie, 'but the sorbet has given me a slight headache.' Perhaps it had; or she was beginning to believe her own lie; or the thought of having sat at the same lunch table as Leopard was the problem.

'I am terribly sorry to hear that,' said the waiter. 'I shall speak to the chef and ensure that in future the sorbet will be served less cold.'

'Thank you,' said Maisie. 'If you will excuse me...'

Once in her cabin, Maisie locked and bolted the door and leaned against it, catching her breath. The room swayed a little and she closed her eyes until the feeling passed. Then she checked the door was securely fastened again, and went to the window to close the curtains.

Something isn't right.

Maisie stopped dead and looked about her. It was nothing obvious; her luggage was where she had left it, the overnight case unlocked and her dressing-case locked. But when she opened her overnight case she could not be sure that everything was exactly as it had been when Ruth had packed it.

It has travelled in a carriage and a train, she told herself. *Things will have moved.* She rummaged amongst the contents, trying to remember what Ruth had put in. Nothing appeared to be missing. In any case, she had packed nothing of a suspicious nature.

But I can't be sure.

Maisie closed the curtains, sat down, and went through the layers of her skirts. The document was stitched into a pocket on the inside of her over-petticoat, a task on which she had spent a good hour two nights ago. She could feel it through the lining. 'Thank heavens,' she murmured. 'I shall have to sleep in it, at this rate.'

But the steward said there was only one other key, and the guard has it. Maisie dabbed at her forehead, which felt cold and clammy. 'You can't be ill, Maisie,' she told herself. 'Now is not the time.'

I must warn Inspector Hamilton, she thought. *But how?*

CHAPTER 14

That afternoon Maisie made a few sorties to attempt to capture the inspector; but her efforts were in vain. She passed by cabin five, and heard Mr Howarth expounding about the best sort of theodolite, and the most convenient scale to draw a map to, once one was in the field. She tried again an hour later and was rewarded with silence; but when she entered the saloon, the pair were nowhere to be seen. The smoking room was next door. No one was in the corridor, and Maisie put her ear to the door. Sure enough, Mr Howarth was speaking. 'Indeed, Mr Carter, I am sure that you could teach Hamilton here a thing or two. He is wet behind the ears — comparatively speaking, of course. I don't know what they teach them these days.'

Maisie withdrew hastily, biting her lip hard to keep herself from giggling; for if she began, she feared hysterics. She did not allow herself to imagine Inspector Hamilton's face until she was safely back in cabin thirteen.

The afternoon dragged, relieved only by the entrance of the steward, who kept his promise to demonstrate the exact workings of every feature in the cabin. He cranked the window open, plumped the chair cushion, let down the bed and put it back up, and pointed out the location of the call button. 'I won't push it, of course, as I am already here,' he said. 'Now, is there anything else that you wish to know, madam? Would you like me to show you how to fold down the bed again?'

'No, no, that's quite all right,' said Maisie. 'May I ask what the arrangements are for cleaning the cabins? Does someone come during the day?'

The steward ran his white-gloved finger along the nearest gleaming teak surface, and inspected it. 'Is there a problem, madam?'

'Oh no, the cabin is spotless,' Maisie gabbled. 'I just — wondered.'

The steward rocked on his heels, clearly delighted to answer a real question. 'We check the cabins and dust them every day, madam, while our passengers are either at lunch or dinner.'

'Oh, then that explains it,' said Maisie.

The steward frowned. 'I don't understand, madam. On departure days we make sure the cabins are clean and in good order before the passengers board. Your cabin will not require cleaning until tomorrow.'

'In that case,' said Maisie, 'I must be mistaken. You say the guard has the key?'

'That's right, madam,' said the steward, 'and he is jolly

careful with them, I can tell you. He counts them all out and back in again every time we perform a round of the cabins.' He smiled proudly. 'Like a well-oiled machine.'

'I'm sure you are,' said Maisie.

Once the steward had gone Maisie bolted the door, set up the writing desk, and ripped a strip of paper from the magazine she had brought with her. On it she wrote: *Please come to cabin late this evening if possible. V worried. Knock twice. M.* She rolled the strip into a little pellet.

When the bell rang for dinner Maisie did not move. She left it a full ten minutes then rose, tidied her hair, and made a hurried entrance into the dining room. 'I'm so sorry I'm late,' she told the waiter. 'I was taking a nap for my headache and I must have overslept. I dreamt that I was late for dinner at home, and when I woke, it was your dinner bell!'

'Oh dear, madam,' said the waiter. 'Never mind. Your table is ready, and we always give our passengers a few minutes' grace.'

He set off at pace and Maisie followed in his wake, moving rather unsteadily. Would the inspector and Mr Howarth be at the same table? Her gaze roved around the tables, seeking him. There he was, studying the menu. She coughed, and the inspector looked up. 'Excuse me,' she said as her hip caught the table and the cutlery rattled. The impact made Maisie wobble, and she stumbled. In reaching out to save herself, she dropped her bag.

'Oh dear,' she said, and knelt to get it. 'I think it is under your seat.' She felt about with a hand, but encountered only the inspector's shoe, into which she tucked her little note.

She heard a creak. 'Here, I have it,' said the inspector's voice. Maisie emerged from her rummagings and Inspector Hamilton handed her the bag with a composed face. 'You could have asked the waiter to get it, Miss Frobisher.'

'Oh yes, I suppose I could. How silly of me.' Maisie brushed herself down, and continued on her way.

Dinner was on an even larger scale than lunch. Maisie chose roast chicken followed by sponge cake and custard; good solid food which could not give her any trouble, as she said to the rest of the table. She toyed with her food while listening to the Carters reminisce about Randolph's various posts in different parts of India; they seemed to have left not an inch of the country unexplored. She could not wait for the meal to finish, but coffee and petit fours followed, with more desultory chat.

There was no sign of any further disturbance when Maisie returned to her room and settled to wait. *The inspector will probably visit the smoking room after dinner*, she thought. She doubted that Mr Howarth would permit him to relax in the saloon; not when so much more knowledge of surveying could be imparted. She yawned, a real one this time. It might well be a long night.

Maisie's eyes were closing when two light taps at the door startled her awake. She unbolted the door and opened it a crack.

'Yes, it is me,' muttered the inspector. 'Quickly.'

He moved noiselessly to the curtained window. Maisie closed and bolted the door and followed him. Inspector

Hamilton bent, and put his mouth to her ear. 'What is it?' he whispered, his breath warm.

'Someone has entered my cabin and gone through my things, I'm almost sure of it,' Maisie whispered back. 'It felt — wrong — when I returned after lunch. And — and I think Leopard is on the train.'

'On the train?' Inspector Hamilton stared at her, aghast.

Maisie swallowed her rising panic. 'The man sitting opposite me at dinner — Mr Ainsley — was talking about shooting leopards, and he gave me a look.' She shivered. 'I can't describe it, but it was as if he could see right through me.'

'Damn,' said the inspector quietly, but with feeling. 'I did not expect this so soon.' He paused, and frowned. 'But if he boarded the train at Bombay, then why bring you all the way to Calcutta?'

'I don't know,' said Maisie. 'Perhaps it fits in with his plans.'

'I don't think I've seen this Ainsley,' said the inspector. 'Can you describe him?'

'I should think he is in his sixties,' said Maisie, 'and he has a sallow face and beady dark eyes. I have only seen him sitting down, but he is broad-shouldered and appears powerfully built.'

'I shall watch for him,' the inspector murmured. 'In the smoking room, and the saloon, and anywhere else I can find him. If you can, keep close to other people. Don't give him a chance to get you alone.' He put out a hand and gently drew Maisie towards him. 'I won't let anything happen to you.'

'Thank you,' whispered Maisie. 'I don't know why he worries me so.'

'If he *is* Leopard, you are right to be worried.' He paused. 'I can hear your heart pounding.' He drew her closer still. 'What were you saying about your cabin —'

They sprang apart at three sharp raps on the door. Both stared at it, and Maisie's hand found the inspector's.

Three more raps, and this time they were followed by a low, angry voice. 'I know you're in there, Hamilton. Open this door right away, or I shall raise the alarm.'

'Oh, for heaven's sake,' said Inspector Hamilton. He strode across the room, unbolted the door, and flung it open to reveal Mr Howarth, his fists clenched and a furious expression on his face.

Mr Howarth stalked in, then rather spoiled the effect of his entrance by closing the door very quietly behind him. 'So this is how you go for a smoke,' he said, with a sneer on his face. 'I looked for you in the smoking room, and in the saloon, and where do I find you? In a young lady's cabin in the dead of night! You had better have a good explanation for this, or else I shall summon the guard and have you thrown off the train. And you needn't expect to spend a moment longer in the Service when I explain this to the viceroy.' His sneer became almost a snarl. 'Now out with it, before I really lose my temper.'

CHAPTER 15

'It isn't what you think, Mr Howarth,' said the inspector.

'I don't know what to think,' retorted Mr Howarth, keeping his voice low with difficulty. 'What should a man think when he finds his colleague in a lady's room? What would *you* think?'

'I know what it looks like,' said the inspector.

Mr Howarth snorted. '"Met a few times at Government House", indeed!' He rounded on Maisie. 'What do you have to say for yourself, Miss Frobisher?'

Maisie took a step back, racking her brains for a suitable response. She opened her mouth, and closed it again.

'At least *she* has the grace to remain silent,' said Mr Howarth. 'You are not paid to sneak around and — and canoodle on the company's time, Mr Hamilton.' He paused, studying both their faces. 'Very well. Since I am to have no explanation, I have no choice but to summon the guard —'

'No!' cried Maisie. She dashed across the cabin and stood in front of the call button. 'You'll have to move me first.'

Mr Howarth shrugged. 'There are other buttons.'

'No,' said Inspector Hamilton. 'You don't understand. The truth of the matter is —' He pushed his hair back from his brow. 'The truth of the matter is — and I am aware this is somewhat irregular — that Miss Frobisher and I are married.'

'What?' cried Mr Howarth, and Maisie felt as if he were speaking her thoughts aloud.

'We met in London a few months ago, when I was on furlough. I knew that I should not marry, certainly given the post I would be returning to, but we could not bear to wait. So we agreed to marry in secret, in a registry office, and to take our chances.' Inspector Hamilton crossed the room and put an arm round Maisie. 'I asked a friend in the Service to put in a good word for me, and he managed to get me transferred to Bombay, into a post where I could support a wife.' He looked at Maisie. 'We came out on the same ship; but this is the first chance we have had to be together since we arrived.'

'Good heavens,' said Mr Howarth. Maisie could sense his mind working, weighing up Inspector Hamilton's story.

She heaved a long sigh while she searched for words to confirm the inspector's story. 'It is . . . a relief that someone else knows at last,' she said quietly. 'It has been such a burden to carry alone.'

'I'm so sorry, darling,' murmured Inspector Hamilton. 'I should have thought more of you.'

'I'm sorry to complain,' said Maisie, gazing up at him. 'It has been terribly hard for you too.'

Mr Howarth coughed, and appeared rather embarrassed. 'You can see how it would look to someone who was . . . unaware of the circumstances.' He put his hands behind his back. 'I must inform the governor of this, of course, as soon as we get to Calcutta.' He cleared his throat. 'I don't suppose you have your marriage certificate with you, Hamilton?'

The inspector shook his head. 'It is locked away in my bank in London,' he said. 'I couldn't risk bringing it with me, and having it found.' He looked shamefaced. 'I would have owned up before now, sir, but I wanted to find my feet first.'

'Quite,' said Mr Howarth. 'I can't say I approve, but there's nothing that can be done about it. However, you are employed in the Indian Civil Service, Hamilton, and as such I consider that your primary duty is to them. Therefore I shall continue to treat you as if you were not married.' He consulted his watch. 'Now, it is past midnight, and we have many more aspects of surveying to go through tomorrow, or you will never be ready for your task. I strongly recommend that you get some sleep.'

'Please,' said Maisie, laying her hand on the inspector's shirt front, 'might we have just five more minutes?'

Mr Howarth didn't seem quite sure where to look. 'Very well. Five minutes, and not a second more.' He laid his hand on the door handle, then paused. 'I'm sorry if I frightened you, Miss Frobisher, but I was angry, and, well…'

'Yes, of course, Mr Howarth,' said Maisie. 'I'm sorry that you had to find out in this way.'

He nodded, and carefully opened the door. 'Five minutes.'

Maisie waited until his footsteps had receded before risking speech. 'You idiot!' she whispered in the inspector's ear. 'Why on earth did you say that?'

'What was I supposed to do?' the inspector whispered back. 'He'd have had me thrown off the train otherwise, and possibly you too.'

'But what if he checks up on us?'

'I'll wire the governor at Calcutta,' said the inspector. 'He'll be able to sort out a fake marriage certificate, or an entry in a register somewhere.' He grinned. 'I suspect that once we get to Calcutta Mr Howarth will be too busy impressing the viceroy to worry about what I'm doing.'

'I hope so,' said Maisie. 'What do I call you, for heaven's sake? I don't even know if you're going by your real first name here.'

'I am,' said Inspector Hamilton. 'We should probably have discussed that before we got married.'

'Yes we should, *Fraser*.' The inspector looked down at her with a pleased, yet curious expression which dissolved Maisie's frown completely. 'Don't for one minute think I approve of this,' she whispered, 'but we had better begin behaving like a newly-married couple before Mr Howarth returns.'

'What a good idea, Maisie,' said the inspector, and

kissed her.

***

Maisie woke with a start. 'It is today,' she murmured. The train was due to arrive in Calcutta before lunchtime, and she felt completely unprepared.

Maisie had spent the previous day alternately wondering what Inspector Hamilton was learning, and avoiding spending any time alone with Mr Ainsley. He had attempted to catch her in the saloon once or twice, and even hurried after her when lunch had finished, but each time Maisie had managed to get away, making excuses which sounded increasingly desperate and flimsy to her own ears.

Instead she had spent time in the company of the Carters and also Miss Price, a tall thin tweed-clad lady of about forty-five who demonstrated such a deep disgust for all things Indian that Maisie couldn't understand why she was there. Listening to that lady's various complaints got her through the hours, and Mrs Carter's good-natured responses provided excellent practice in keeping a straight face.

Maisie had managed to meet with the inspector just once. Mr Howarth had approached her in the saloon after dinner and said, grudgingly, that if she wished he could spare Mr Hamilton for ten minutes at nine o'clock. 'No more than that, mind,' he said, looking as if he wanted to wag a finger at her. 'He will be meeting with the Viceroy tomorrow, and I cannot let personal partiality hinder the Service.' Maisie could actually hear the capital letters.

True to his word, Mr Howarth duly delivered the

inspector to cabin thirteen at nine o'clock sharp. 'Now I shall go for a smoke,' he said, 'and when my pipe is out, your time is up.'

'Thank you, sir,' said Inspector Hamilton. 'I appreciate it.'

'No need to thank me,' said Mr Howarth gruffly, and beat a hasty retreat.

'No word from Leopard, I take it,' the inspector murmured in Maisie's ear.

'If Ainsley is Leopard,' said Maisie, 'he tried to get me alone several times, but I evaded him.'

'I don't think he is, you know,' said the inspector. 'Even less so, now I've seen him.'

'Then what is he doing?' asked Maisie. 'You must admit his conduct is suspicious.'

'Perhaps he will leave you his fortune,' said the inspector. 'You have taken his fancy, and he has no one else to leave it to.'

'Much as I like that idea,' said Maisie, 'I don't think that's the answer.' She sighed. 'What shall we do tomorrow? What if Leopard doesn't communicate with us?'

'Then I shall go to the reception at the viceroy's, and I suppose after that I shall do some surveying work for him, or at least something to keep Howarth off my back,' said the inspector. 'You can explore Calcutta, and I'm sure that you will be welcome at Government House too.'

Maisie sighed. 'That isn't what I came for.'

'Why did you come to India, Maisie?' Inspector Hamilton's face wore an expression of honest puzzlement.

'You said that you wanted to see something different...'

'I wanted to get away,' said Maisie. 'I was so tired of my old life. It was all parties and balls and dinners and not being taken seriously.' She looked up at him. 'Just for once, I wanted to be taken seriously.'

A smile flickered across the inspector's face. 'I can assure you that I take you very seriously indeed,' he said, advancing towards her.

'But what do we *do*?' asked Maisie, submitting to his embrace rather impatiently. 'Do I advertise in a Calcutta newspaper, or wait? Surely something will happen.'

'Something is certain to happen,' said the inspector, kissing the top of her head. 'That's what I'm afraid of, Maisie.'

Shortly afterwards Mr Howarth had come to collect his charge. 'I'm afraid you must get used to this, Miss Frobisher,' he said. 'We shall be busy men in Calcutta, and no doubt absent for days at a time when we are out surveying. You will have to cultivate your patience.'

'I believe I have already done that,' Maisie had replied, injecting as much frost into the comment as she possibly could.

And today they would arrive in Calcutta. Maisie yawned, made herself ready for the day, and proceeded to the dining car at a leisurely pace. Breakfast, no doubt, would be as gargantuan a meal as the day before; but if she could eat now, at least she would have something to sustain her later, when her nerves would really be stretched. She passed the inspector and Mr Howarth on the way to her table, and noted with amusement that the inspector was tackling a large plate of kedgeree. Clearly his thoughts were running on the same lines as hers.

'Ah, Miss Frobisher,' said Mr Ainsley, with a gleam in his eye. 'I had given you up for lost.'

'I overslept,' said Maisie, taking her seat.

'Ah, sleep that knits up the ravelled sleeve of care,' said Mr Ainsley. 'I wouldn't mind some of that myself, but I am a light sleeper. Once I wake I find it difficult to drift off, so I am a watcher in the night.' Again his bright black eyes found hers.

'I shall have toast, two boiled eggs, and a pot of tea,' said Maisie.

'Are you ready to disembark, Miss Frobisher?' asked Mrs Carter.

'Once I have packed a few things, yes,' said Maisie.

'Jolly good,' said Mrs Carter. 'I packed everything last night. I always worry that I shall be taken unawares in the morning, with clothes everywhere and not enough room in my case.'

The rest of the meal proceeded peacefully and Maisie made a quick escape, pleading her packing. Twenty minutes later the steward knocked on her door. 'We shall be arriving in Calcutta in one hour precisely, madam. If you have packing to do, it would be best to begin now,' he said, as if Maisie's packed and strapped cases were invisible.

'I think I'm ready,' said Maisie. 'Thank you for looking after me.'

'It has been a pleasure, madam,' he said. 'I hope that you have a safe onward journey.' And with that he bowed, and disappeared.

Maisie sat in her folding chair and sighed. So close to her destination, with no idea of what would happen next. *I do not even have a place to stay*, she thought. *I should have asked the steward to recommend a hotel.* She comforted herself with the thought that there would be a hotel near the railway station, or at least someone who could direct her to one.

Maisie closed her eyes and let the strange journey wash over her; the plains and trees and hills and mountains flashing by outside, the British food served by Indian waiters, the people she had met, and the ridiculous scene with the inspector only two nights ago. *Married, indeed*, she said to herself, and managed to blush and giggle at the same time.

Suddenly a scratching noise made Maisie open her eyes. An envelope was working its way underneath the door. Maisie grasped it and pulled, and as she did so footsteps thundered away. She gasped and wrenched at the bolt, but by the time she had unlocked the door and stuck her head out, whoever had delivered the note was long gone. *Miss Frobisher* was written on the envelope, in neat printing just like the hand which had addressed her ticket.

Maisie closed her door, drew the bolt, and opened the note.

The time is near. 8 pm at the pyramid, South Park Street Cemetery, on the Lower Circular Road. Soon we shall see the colour of each other's fur. L

CHAPTER 16

As the train pulled into Howrah Station, Maisie's first sight of Calcutta should have been truly impressive. But she had no eyes for her surroundings; no eyes for anything except the inspector and her message. Maisie was standing at the door of the carriage with her cases well before the train had stopped, and the other passengers grumbled at having to stand further down the corridor.

At long last the train ground to a halt. Maisie wrenched open the carriage door and got herself and her luggage onto the platform more by happy accident than design. She hefted her cases and set off purposefully to where she thought cabin five would disembark. A porter ran after her shouting 'Miss! Miss!' But Maisie marched on, her breath coming rather faster than usual, looking for a tall dark man in a Panama hat. There was no shortage of these on the train, and Maisie weaved between various groups, peering into faces in a manner which, if someone had done it to her, she would have found extremely rude. This, she judged, was no time for politeness.

At length she found not the inspector but Mr Howarth, standing by his battered portmanteau and the inspector's case. 'I take it you are not looking for me,' he said, wryly. 'If it is Mr Hamilton you seek, he has returned to the carriage to *fetch something*.' His tone indicated extreme scepticism. 'I'm sure he will be most surprised to find you here when he emerges.'

'So what are your plans for the rest of the day, Mr Howarth?' asked Maisie, deciding that ignoring his sarcasm was easier than reacting to it.

'Strictly business, Miss Frobisher,' said Mr Howarth sternly. 'First to our hotel, to unpack and get our dress clothes ready for the evening, then a light meal before I brief Mr Hamilton on what we shall say to the viceroy tonight. There is no second chance to make a first impression, you know.'

'Did I hear the name Frobisher?' Maisie turned to see a tall, equine man, beautifully dressed in a cream linen suit so spotless that it appeared brand-new. He smiled at her, and his eyes crinkled.

'Why yes, I am Miss Frobisher,' she said.

'Then I have had a stroke of luck,' he said, and drew a small bundle of cards from his pocket. He thumbed through them and presented Maisie with one.

His Excellency the Viceroy of India
invites Miss Maisie Frobisher to

a reception at Government House.
Monday 30th October, 7-9 pm
Formal dress

'Thank you,' said Maisie, beaming. 'Is white muslin considered formal dress here?'

The gentleman's smile broadened. 'For the ladies, yes. Alas, we men must confine ourselves to tail suits.'

Maisie could not help laughing, not so much at the joke but at Mr Howarth's expression, which was hovering between respect for the official and annoyance that Maisie would be at the reception.

The carriage door opened and Inspector Hamilton came out, looking rather hot and bothered. 'There you are,' he said to Maisie. 'I knew I had a book of yours to return, and I have been seeking you all over the train.' He pulled a cheap paperback from his pocket and gave it to Maisie.

'I had completely forgotten,' said Maisie, stuffing the book in her bag, for she was fairly sure Mr Howarth would not believe that she had lent the inspector her copy of *Montezuma's Daughter*. 'In any case, I could have reminded you at the reception tonight.'

'Oh, are you going?' the inspector said casually.

'I am indeed, Mr Hamilton,' said Maisie. 'This kind gentleman has just issued me with an invitation.'

'Then I shall see you there,' said the inspector. 'Shall we make a move, Howarth? I believe you wanted to get to the Imperial Hotel by twelve o'clock, and it is already a quarter to.'

'Yes,' snapped Mr Howarth, 'and you have kept *me*

waiting.' He picked up his portmanteau, took a guidebook from his pocket, and with a jerk of his head to Inspector Hamilton, walked off.

'Hamilton, did you say?' asked the gentleman, paging through his cards. 'Surveyor chap?'

'That would be me,' said Inspector Hamilton.

'Yes, here we are.' He handed the inspector a card. 'I am Captain James, by the way, one of the viceroy's many minions.' He glanced down the platform, where Mr Howarth was now merely a speck among many others. 'Who was the other gentleman?'

'That was Mr Howarth, my . . . colleague,' said Inspector Hamilton.

Captain James went through his pile, then licked his finger and went through it again. 'Strange,' he said, 'I don't seem to have a card for him. Although if he is usually that snappish, perhaps it is as well. I shall see *you* tonight.' He bestowed another charming smile on them, and strolled off.

'I thought he'd never go,' said Maisie. 'Leopard has written. The pyramid, South Park Street cemetery, tonight at eight.'

The inspector whistled. 'He doesn't hang about, does he? Well, we can slip out of the reception and find a carriage. I doubt the dress code includes guns, but it's best that we are both prepared.' He grimaced. 'The hardest part will probably be giving Howarth the slip.'

Maisie frowned. 'Yes. But how odd…'

'What's odd?' said the inspector. 'I had better go, before Howarth returns and drags me to the hotel himself.'

'We must say our goodbyes first,' said Maisie, loudly. She stood on tiptoe and whispered in his ear, 'That there is no invitation for Mr Howarth.' She kissed the inspector's cheek for good measure, and stood back.

'Probably an administrative error,' said the inspector, laughing. 'Now, you disgraceful lady, you had better go and get your luggage, or you will be a crumpled specimen when you meet the viceroy tonight.' He grinned. 'At least you will finally see a pyramid, Maisie.' He strolled down the platform as if he had not a care in the world, and Maisie watched him go.

***

Government House in Calcutta was very different from its Bombay equivalent, but superbly grand nevertheless. Maisie had had her muslin pressed and taken considerable pains with her hair, but even so, as her carriage rolled down the long drive towards the classical facade, she hoped that she would not be too out of place.

However, once she had ascended the steps it was not so different from the governor's reception at Bombay; attentive aides-de-camp, champagne and nibbles, though these ones were Indian rather than British in character. Maisie accepted a samosa gratefully and bit into it with extreme care.

'Miss Frobisher!' It was Mrs Carter, pinker and plumper than ever in a bright green dress, towing Mr Carter behind her. 'I did wonder if we would see you. I told Randolph that I thought you would be invited, but I didn't like to say anything in case you weren't.'

'Well, here I am,' laughed Maisie. 'And excited, as this

is my first one. I suppose you have attended many.'

'Oh yes, too many to count,' said Mrs Carter, accepting a glass of champagne from the waiter. 'But it's still fun.'

'May I join in?' Inspector Hamilton appeared at Maisie's elbow, dapper in white tie and tails.

'But of course,' said Maisie. 'Mr Hamilton, may I introduce Mr and Mrs Carter. Mr Hamilton will be surveying for the viceroy,' she added. 'We know each other slightly from Bombay.'

'Oh, how nice,' said Mrs Carter. 'Have you visited Calcutta before, Mr Hamilton?' And she launched into a stream of chatter which was only interrupted by a call of silence for the viceroy.

As they turned to welcome their host Maisie felt a light touch on her arm, and Inspector Hamilton drew her a few steps away. 'They wouldn't let him in,' he muttered, with barely-disguised satisfaction. 'I was almost sorry for him.'

'That makes things much easier for us,' said Maisie. 'It is a quarter past seven now. We can get ourselves introduced, then slip out. The cemetery is a mile and a half from here; I checked at the hotel.'

'Good thinking,' said the inspector. 'This afternoon I was so bored by his surveying talk, and so taken up with planning how to escape from him, that the thought of what comes afterwards barely crossed my mind.' Another cry for silence rang out, and they hastily composed themselves.

The viceroy, Lord Strathcairn, was a tall, stooped man in rather the same pattern as Lord Montgomery, except for a flourishing military moustache. His voice reached easily to the back of the Banquet Hall. 'Welcome to Calcutta, one and all. I hope you will find your time here pleasant and productive. But for tonight we shall put thoughts of productivity aside, and enjoy ourselves.'

'I like him,' whispered Maisie.

'There is much to admire and to enjoy about India; but also much to do. Health, education, and public works can be improved. It is my job to make sure that they are, and many of you will be in a position to help me.' Was it Maisie's imagination, or did the viceroy's eyes meet hers? *A public speaker's trick*, she thought, and continued to listen.

'I shall meet with many of you in the days, weeks and even months to follow, in our quest for a better India; an India where British and Indians can work together in harmony, for the greater good.'

There was muttering at that, and Maisie saw a group of richly-dressed Indians speaking urgently amongst themselves. The viceroy looked in their direction. 'Part of this will be giving greater representation to Indian interests. That will not happen tonight; but it is a promise for the future.' This seemed to satisfy the group, who nodded vehemently. 'I shall aim to speak to as many of you as possible, but if I do not manage to reach you, I can assure you it is a question of capacity rather than inclination. On that note, please enjoy yourselves.' He stepped back, and a wave of applause echoed around the room.

'He's different, isn't he?' murmured Maisie.

'I wonder what the governor makes of him,' said Inspector Hamilton. 'And what he makes of the governor.

Let's see if we can approach the venerable presence.'

They managed to make modest progress, but the room was so densely packed that it required several apologies to move a foot in any direction. The inspector checked his watch. 'It is half past seven already,' he said. 'We must go, or we shall be late.'

Maisie eyed the crowds; the nearest door was twenty feet away. 'Could you get me a glass of water, please?' she said, in a carrying voice. 'I think I might faint.' She swayed, and the inspector caught her just in time.

Maisie kept her eyes closed as she was half-dragged from the room. 'Fresh air, that's all I need,' she murmured. She only opened her eyes when the warm, humid air of outside breathed on her face.

'I wish I could play a trick like that,' said the inspector, and hailed a carriage.

The journey was short; too short for Maisie's liking. Inspector Hamilton held her hand, and murmured words of reassurance the whole way, but she still felt sick. 'I shall stay as close as I can,' he said. 'Excuse me a moment.' He turned, and appeared to be fiddling with his shirt. Eventually he extracted a folded length of material which turned out to be a short, thin black cloak, and wrapped it round himself, hiding his white waistcoat and shirt-front.

'Very good,' said Maisie. 'Do you have a rabbit in your hat as well?'

'Not today.' He leaned over and kissed Maisie on the mouth. 'Do you have it with you?'

'The gun? Of course,' said Maisie, feeling breathless.

'I meant the document,' he murmured.

'Yes; that too.'

'Good. Remember, you are more important than any document. If you need to hand it over, just do it.' He kissed her again. '"Rabbit" can be our code word. If you are worried for your safety, drop it into the conversation, and I shall come as fast as I can. Or use my gun, if I have to.'

Maisie swallowed. 'I hope you won't have to.'

The inspector looked grim. 'So do I.'

'Nearly there,' shouted the driver. Maisie saw iron railings, and the driver pulled up outside a gate. 'Most people visit in the day,' he said.

'You get down, Maisie,' said the inspector. 'I shall pay the driver, then follow.'

The gate was secured with a chain and padlock; but not five feet away someone had bent the railings so that a small person could creep through without difficulty. She crouched, and wriggled through.

At the pyramid, the note had said. Maisie walked carefully through the overgrown grass, skirting the graves. There were no lights, but the moon hung pale and impassive in the sky, throwing everything into sharp relief. Maisie saw a forest of crosses and monuments, and hurried towards it. Sure enough, among them was a pyramid, fenced round with a low iron railing; but the gate was open. Maisie approached it, her heart in her mouth.

'Come in, do.' Maisie checked a scream. The voice seemed to issue from the pyramid itself. A low laugh. 'Do not be afraid.'

Slowly Maisie walked forward, willing her legs to carry her. She could make out something moving in the shadow of the doorway. 'You are oddly dressed for a panther.' The figure showed itself briefly, then stepped back. 'I expected a fur cape at the very least.'

Maisie laughed, then checked herself hastily, for she knew that if she continued she would not stop.

'I'm sorry I couldn't find somewhere more cheerful to meet,' the voice continued. 'But Calcutta is busy at this time of night, and it is nice and quiet here.'

Maisie found her voice. 'Leopard?'

'The same.' The voice sounded amused. 'Why don't you come and say hello?'

Won't you walk into my parlour, said the spider to the fly. Maisie hoped beyond hope that the inspector was near. She took another step, then another. As she drew closer she saw that the figure was wrapped in a long black cloak, with a muffler covering most of his face, and a hat pulled low. He was fair-skinned, and from his voice, British, but she could not say more than that.

'So, Panther, we meet at last.' The figure did not step forward; rather, he lounged in the doorway to the tomb. The moon barely reached the entrance, but there was sufficient light for Maisie to see him raise a gloved hand to his muffler and pull it down. 'A very good evening to you,' he said, and took a step forward.

Maisie gasped, and it was some time before she could find words. 'Mr Howarth…?'

CHAPTER 17

'Have I surprised you, Miss Frobisher?' Mr Howarth smiled.

'Just slightly,' said Maisie. 'I thought you were...' She paused, unable to put what she was feeling into words.

'On the level? A straight bat?' The scorn he put into those words was immeasurable. 'One of those old-school gentlemen who plays the game?'

'All those things,' said Maisie.

'Are you disappointed?' asked Mr Howarth. He seemed genuinely interested in her response.

'I'm really not sure.' Maisie goggled at him. 'But if you're Leopard, why did you bring me here, when we could have met in Bombay with much less trouble?'

'I have my reasons,' Mr Howarth said airily. 'Now, to business. Do you have the document?'

Maisie took a deep breath before responding. 'Yes. Yes,

I do.' Her mind was racing. Mr Howarth, the mole! The source of all the trouble! *I must get him to say something incriminating*, she thought. 'Did you know Miss Jeroboam?' she asked.

'I did not,' said Mr Howarth. 'But I recruited her.'

'So you approached her in London?' said Maisie. 'How? Were you on leave?'

'I do not mean physically,' said Mr Howarth impatiently. 'I suggested her as a potential operative, one who would be above suspicion. I had read of her exploits — and the criticism in the more conservative newspapers. I had also noted that she was not a Fellow of any Society despite her achievements. A respected, brave, resourceful young lady, yet still rejected by the establishment. I thought she would resent that enough to be worth a gamble, and I was right. Now, am I right about you?'

Maisie stared at him. The situation was so far from what she had imagined, in that Mr Howarth was part of it, that she found it hard to remember her manners. 'What is your opinion of me, Mr Howarth?'

'It is too early to say,' said Mr Howarth, after studying her for some time. 'You are a wealthy young lady who can think clearly and act a part, as you demonstrated when I surprised you and Mr Hamilton in your cabin the other night.'

'What do you mean?' said Maisie, with a sinking feeling.

'I mean that you two are no more married than I am,' said Mr Howarth, smugly. 'Hamilton is far too sensible, and, dare I say, self-interested, to indulge in a clandestine marriage.' He smiled. 'Do not worry, Miss Frobisher, I shall say nothing to anyone about the matter. You may have your fun. Regrettably, though, that little episode suggests to me that you are inclined to follow your heart rather than your head, and that is hardly suitable behaviour for one of our people.'

'But you recruited Miss Jeroboam based on what you thought her emotions would be,' said Maisie.

Mr Howarth considered. 'Partly, but I also thought that a handsome sum of money without humiliation attached would be an attractive inducement for Miss Jeroboam.' His eyes seemed to bore through Maisie. 'Are you prepared to take her place? To travel where you are sent, taking and using information as you are directed?'

Maisie met his eyes, and did her best not to flinch. 'What is the purpose of your activity, Leopard?'

'It suits me,' said Mr Howarth. 'I enjoy the work, and I am well paid for it when it comes my way. I wish it to come my way more often. More than that you do not need to know, at present.'

'Could I consider your question?' asked Maisie. 'I do not wish to give you an answer in this strange place and regret it later. I feel like a rabbit in a field of traps, uncertain which way to go.' She forced herself to keep her eyes on Mr Howarth.

'I don't see why not,' he replied. 'But before you leave, please hand over the document in your possession. I have waited long enough.'

Maisie hesitated, then remembered Inspector

Hamilton's words: *You are more important than any document.* 'I shall,' she said. She opened her bag and retrieved the little oilskin packet.

Mr Howarth's eyes gleamed, and he almost snatched the packet from her hand. He stepped into the moonlight to scrutinise the document, and Maisie took the opportunity to look past him at the cemetery. *Where is the inspector? Will he shoot Mr Howarth, or overpower him? If so, now is the time to do it.*

'Excellent,' said Mr Howarth. 'I must congratulate you, Miss Frobisher. I am sure no one suspected you, a delightful young lady, of such a deed.' He folded the document carefully, slipped it into its covering, and put it in an inner pocket. 'I suppose now you want your reward, Panther.' He rummaged within his cloak.

'I — I —' stammered Maisie. Then she fell silent; for Mr Howarth was pointing a gleaming revolver at her.

'Take a step back, Miss Frobisher,' he said. 'That's right. You will find that the door opens easily.'

'Help!' screamed Maisie. 'Help me!' *Where is Fraser?*

'You may scream as loud as you like,' said Mr Howarth, and the gun never wavered. 'There is no one here who will help you. People think the cemetery is full of ghosts, and they will assume you are an unquiet spirit. As perhaps you are.' He smirked. 'I have had men watching since well before you arrived. I instructed them to look out for your friend Mr Hamilton, and — take care of him. I do not anticipate any further trouble from him.'

'No!' cried Maisie.

Mr Howarth put his free hand to his mouth and

whistled. 'Don't worry,' he said confidingly, 'I didn't tell them to kill him. Where would be the fun in that?'

Maisie heard rustling and then two men appeared, carrying a limp burden wrapped in cloth.

'Miss Frobisher, if you wouldn't mind opening the door,' said Mr Howarth.

'But you can't —'

'Yes, I can. In case you hadn't realised, Miss Frobisher, you have admitted your guilt, and that of your friend, out of your own mouth. You have handed me a document which you really shouldn't have, revealed to me that you know Miss Jeroboam's part in this affair, and showed willingness to attempt further espionage. The viceroy will be extremely interested in what I have to tell him, don't you think?' He gestured with the revolver. 'Open that door, Miss Frobisher, for I shall not ask so nicely again.'

'It's a mistake!' said Maisie. 'You don't understand —'

'Oh, I do.' Mr Howarth moved his gun meaningly.

Shaking, Maisie did as she was told. She could see nothing within the tomb; there were no windows, and it was pitch black.

'That's it. Now step inside.'

'You can't leave us here!'

'I don't intend to,' said Mr Howarth. 'Not for too long, anyway. Just as long as it takes for me to obtain an audience with the viceroy. He didn't want to let me into his little reception tonight, you know. I can't think why.'

'You weren't meant to be there,' said Maisie.

'No, I wasn't,' said Mr Howarth. 'When I engage in spy-catching I do it independently. I don't toady to the governor for a special surveying assignment, or dress like a fashion plate to impress people. Some of us have to rely on our wits.' He spoke to the men, but not in English. 'Move back, Miss Frobisher, or there will be no room for your friend.'

Maisie slid her foot backwards, feeling smooth paving, and stretched her hand behind her. She didn't meet with a wall, or — worse.

'There, that wasn't so hard, was it? And again, please.' Mr Howarth sounded rather bored with the proceedings. He barked another order to the men, who brought their bundle forward and put it, none too gently, into the tomb.

'Goodbye, Miss Frobisher; or should I say *au revoir.*' Mr Howarth grinned at her. 'I daresay I shall see you both at the trial, assuming you live that long.' The last thing Maisie saw was his arm reaching forward before the door clanged shut, and the key turned in the lock. Then a rattle as the key was withdrawn, a low chuckle, and silence.

Maisie knelt by the motionless bundle on the floor and unwrapped it. She touched it cautiously, encountering a knee, then explored until she found the inspector's hand, and his head. 'Still warm,' she murmured. She felt for blood and found none, then kissed his unresponsive lips. 'Wake up, Fraser,' she pleaded, and her voice cracked. 'Don't leave me alone in here.' She waited for a motion, a noise, for anything except the sound of his breathing, but nothing came. She sighed, and manoeuvred herself so that his head was in her lap. *When he comes round,* she told herself, *I shall have a better idea of what to do.* She stroked his hair, and stared into the darkness, and waited.

CHAPTER 18

Maisie finished the lullaby she was singing and racked her brains for another tune. *Anything to keep the silence out.* A thought popped into her head, and she almost laughed with the absurdity of it. 'It's hardly the season,' she said, 'but never mind,' and launched into 'Silent Night'.

Maisie was beginning the second verse when she felt the inspector shift a little, and then cough. 'Hello, Maisie,' he said. 'I would have thought that I had died and gone to heaven, except that you are no celestial choir.'

'I'm the only celestial choir you're likely to get,' retorted Maisie, before helping him sit up and throwing her arms round him. 'Don't you ever give me a scare like that again, Fraser Hamilton.'

'I'll try not to,' he said. 'Where are we?'

'Locked in a tomb,' said Maisie.

'Oh.' A silence. 'That isn't promising.'

'What do you remember?' asked Maisie.

'Not much,' the inspector replied. 'I had just got myself to a place with a good view of the pyramid, and after that, nothing. As I have an aching head, I can guess what came next.' She could feel him looking at her. 'I take it that it didn't go well.'

'So you didn't see who Leopard was?'

'No, I didn't.' He paused. 'Was it that Ainsley chap?'

'I wish it had been,' said Maisie. 'It was Mr Howarth, and he wasn't Leopard. He set a trap to catch *us* meeting Leopard. He's got the document, and he's going to the viceroy.'

'Damn,' said the inspector. 'But the document's a fake, anyway. The governor can tell him that. What's more important right now is how we get out.' He got to his feet carefully, and Maisie heard him trying the door. Then he hammered on it, and yelled 'Help! Help!'

'There's no point,' said Maisie. 'No one will be here at this hour.'

An answering bang shook the door. The inspector jumped back and trod on Maisie. 'Ow!' she cried.

'Sorry,' said the inspector, then shouted again. 'Heeeeelp!'

'We are trying to,' said a very reasonable voice. 'Can you hold that torch up a bit, please?'

Maisie stared at the door. 'Would you mind pinching me?' she asked the inspector. 'I might be dreaming.'

'No, I definitely heard that,' said Inspector Hamilton. 'Hello! We are locked in!' he cried.

The lock rattled. 'I don't think this will do it,' said the

voice. 'Stand back and I'll shoot the lock out.'

Maisie and the inspector shuffled back as far as they could, careless now of the contents of their prison.

'Are you standing back?' the voice demanded.

'Yes, we are,' said Maisie.

'Right, then.' A loud bang preceded a scraping, screeching sound, followed by a satisfied exclamation of 'There we are!' The handle turned, and, under the brilliant light of the moon, Maisie found herself looking into the faces of Mr and Mrs Carter.

***

'We had to wait till we were sure everyone had gone,' said Mrs Carter. 'Your prissy friend left very quickly, but the men he'd brought with him took their time. I think they were arguing over money. It took them a good twenty minutes to disperse.'

'But what are you doing here in the first place?' asked Maisie.

'We followed you from the reception,' said Mrs Carter. 'I must say, Miss Frobisher, that while I admire your quick thinking in pretending to faint, you might be more convincing if you were a little paler and slimmer. I usually rely on indigestion.' She smiled encouragingly at Maisie. 'Now, does anyone need brandy?' She rummaged in her bag and produced a hip flask.

'I wouldn't mind,' said Inspector Hamilton. 'It has been a strange evening.'

'Yes, indeed,' said Mrs Carter. 'I wouldn't have had your colleague down as a spy, not in a million years. I'm rather impressed.'

'But he isn't,' said Maisie. 'He was pretending, to get me to incriminate myself. At least —' All the things that had happened since her arrival in India churned in Maisie's brain. The whispering campaign, the polo match, the instruction to wear white muslin, the messages in the newspaper — 'I don't know,' she concluded, pushing her half-down hair off her face.

'If he was legitimate,' said Mrs Carter, 'then why didn't he have the police with him? Locking people up in tombs is hardly government policy.'

'I suppose not,' said Maisie. 'And he wasn't invited to the reception. He mentioned working undercover, but —'

Mrs Carter snorted. 'I work undercover, but you won't find *me* getting turned away at the viceroy's front door.'

'So if he isn't going to the viceroy,' said Maisie, 'where is he going?'

'No idea,' said Mrs Carter. 'I was busy keeping an eye on the tomb and the men. Randolph, you were closer to the gate. Did you spot anything?'

Mr Carter thought. 'He didn't have transport waiting; or if he did, it wasn't nearby. I would have followed him, but I didn't want to leave you alone, Estella.'

'Did you see which way he went?' asked the inspector.

'He was heading towards the main road that goes into the city,' said Mr Carter. 'I caught a glimpse of his face, and he looked extremely pleased with himself.'

'I'm sure he did,' said the inspector grimly.

'Oh, and I heard something,' said Mr Carter. 'Now what was it? He was talking to himself, of course, so it wasn't very distinct —'

'Now do spit it out, Randolph,' said Mrs Carter, comfortably.

'Don't rush me, Estella,' he replied. 'It sounded like Damascus, although why anybody would say that... "Not quite Damascus".'

'Damascus,' said Maisie. 'Isn't that in the Bible?'

Mrs Carter laughed. 'Indeed it is; Paul's conversion took place on the road to Damascus. If you knew Calcutta at all, you'd know exactly where he's going, and it's not half a mile away. He's heading for St Paul's Cathedral, and I doubt it's for a late service.'

***

'What do we do now?' asked Inspector Hamilton.

'What can we do?' said Maisie. 'He's got a head start.'

'That doesn't mean he's finished,' replied Mrs Carter.

'What time is it?' asked Maisie. 'I feel as if we were trapped in that tomb for hours.'

'It was about twenty-five minutes,' said Mrs Carter, consulting her watch. 'It is a quarter to nine, so if he is meeting someone there at nine we still have time. If we hurry, that is. Come on; we have a carriage waiting in a side road. Can you walk, Mr Hamilton, or do you need Randolph to give you an arm?'

'I can walk,' said the inspector, 'but an arm might be a good idea if you want me to move quickly.'

Five minutes later they were in a large closed carriage, speeding down a wide, well-kept road. 'Do you have guns?' asked Mr Carter.

The inspector felt in his jacket. 'They've taken mine.'

'I still have mine,' said Maisie. 'Though I'm not sure

how much use it will be.'

'As long as you can point it at someone and look as if you mean it, that will do,' said Mrs Carter, and pulled a highly-polished pistol from her bag. 'Shame I didn't bring a spare.'

'So . . . is there a plan?' asked Maisie. For the first time she noticed that the Carters were wearing long black cloaks.

Mrs Carter caught her eye. 'Reversible,' she said. 'Very handy for a quick change. Now, as your friend has a gun, I don't propose to approach him directly, and I wouldn't be surprised if whoever he is meeting is armed too. I would assume that the meeting is to hand over the document you gave him —'

'Which is fake,' said Maisie. 'Lord Montgomery gave it to me.'

'Oh, is it?' said Mrs Carter. 'That makes things easier.' She sighed. 'It would be even easier to shoot the pair of them, but I suppose we should keep them alive.' Her face was unreadable in the dark carriage, but Maisie could hear the rise and fall of her voice, the way she was thinking things through. 'A further help is that the cathedral square is a public place. It is lit up at night, and there will be people walking in the gardens and nearby. There is nothing to stop me approaching Howarth as someone I recognise from the train and asking if he knows where you are, Mr Hamilton.'

'I'm not sure I like that, Estella,' said Mr Carter.

'Then think of something better, Randolph,' she replied.

'What about if you do that,' said Maisie, 'and then…' She leaned forward and muttered in Mrs Carter's ear.

'That's interesting,' said Mrs Carter, 'and also rather dangerous. But if we can do that…' She grinned.

'What *are* we going to do?' asked Mr Carter.

'We shall cook Mr Howarth's goose,' said Mrs Carter placidly. 'And I apologise for the mixed metaphor, but as Mrs Beeton doubtless never said, first catch your hare. We'll go through it properly for the benefit of the gentlemen in the party; but we do not have much time.'

CHAPTER 19

Mrs Carter tweaked the blind on her side of the carriage, and regarded the cathedral. 'Excellent. Nice and busy,' she commented. 'But if you don't mind me saying so, you two could do with smartening up before you appear in public. Particularly you, Miss Frobisher.' Maisie winced as Mrs Carter's critical eye passed over her. 'I know it isn't your fault, but you do look a bit of a state. If you could remove what hairpins you have remaining, please.' She retrieved a comb from her bag and eyed Maisie's curls. 'Perhaps not,' Mrs Carter said, and passed the comb to the inspector. She took a ribbon from her bag, plaited Maisie's hair, and twisted it into a neat bun, securing it with the ribbon and hairpins. 'Much tidier,' she said with satisfaction. 'If you take our cloaks, the worst of the damage to your clothes will be hidden. We don't want people staring, do we?'

'No,' said Maisie, feeling as if the tight plait were

pulling the skin back from her face.

Mrs Carter took a pair of opera glasses from her bag and peered out of the window. 'I think I see our man,' she said. 'Medium height, stocky, trying to look inconspicuous and cowering behind a buttress.' She snapped the glasses shut. 'He clearly hasn't done much of this work; anyone could creep up on him and overhear. By anyone, Miss Frobisher, I mean you.' She held up a finger. 'Not yet!' Maisie took her hand from the carriage door. 'We shall wait until Mr Leopard approaches, in case he sneaks up on you sneaking up on our fake Leopard.' She snorted. 'It's like a children's story.'

Maisie checked her watch, which said five minutes past nine. 'Maybe he isn't coming,' she said.

'He will come, Miss Frobisher,' said Mr Carter. 'He's just making our man wait a bit. Getting him nice and nervous.'

The minutes stretched onward, and Maisie had to clasp her hands together to keep herself from fidgeting. She almost wished that Leopard would hurry up and come out, so that she would have something to do besides wait and twitch.

'Could this be our chap?' asked Mr Carter, pointing at a tall, portly man carrying a newspaper, and dressed for the weather in a light suit and straw hat. He approached the cathedral and craned his neck to see the tower, then approached the doorway and examined the carvings.

'Looks likely,' said Mrs Carter, applying her opera glasses to the task. 'Can't say I recognise him.'

She offered the glasses to Maisie, who focused on the

man. 'At least it isn't Mr Ainsley,' she said, giving back the glasses.

'Mr Ainsley?' Mrs Carter began to laugh. 'I shall have so much to tell you later, my dear.'

'What was I supposed to think?' said Maisie, feeling rather aggrieved.

'Never mind all that now,' said Mrs Carter. 'He's walking over.'

The man had taken something from his pocket and was talking to Mr Howarth. 'They're staying put,' said Mrs Carter. 'Off you go, Miss Frobisher — and remember, stay well back.'

Maisie let herself out of the opposite side of the carriage and strolled across the plaza to the furthest side of the cathedral. When she was definitely hidden from the men, she scurried to the rear. Maisie paused to catch her breath, then advanced a few steps at a time. She heard voices, and stopped dead.

'And you're sure no one knows you're here?' The voice had a curious lilt to it. It was the sort of voice that would tell a story, and charm the listener to sleep.

'Absolutely, Leopard,' said Mr Howarth, and Maisie could imagine him puffing himself up.

'Good. Have you managed to obtain it?'

'Yes, I have.' Maisie heard rustling.

'And how did you manage to get it? The newspapers reported Lynx's death at sea.'

'It wasn't easy, I'll admit that.' Uncertainty had crept into Mr Howarth's voice, and he spoke more quickly. 'Lynx passed the document to a friend on the ship before she died. That is how I got it.'

'You haven't given me a full answer, Jackal.' The lilting voice was amused now. 'How did you get the document?'

'I... Lynx's friend revealed to me that she had it, and in my official capacity I took it on behalf of the government. She knows nothing of all this.'

'And she will not ask any awkward questions?'

'Definitely not.' That answer shot out of Mr Howarth.

'That sounds rather final.' A low laugh. 'I do hope you haven't caused a fuss, Jackal.' He paused. 'If you would let me have it?'

A moment's silence, then Mr Howarth said, 'Aren't you going to look at it?'

'What, here?' Another light, easy laugh. 'No, I shall check it over at my leisure. When I am satisfied, I shall get in touch.'

Maisie edged away, then walked out from the shadow of the cathedral and back again, opening her cloak as she did so. She could see the Carters standing perhaps twenty feet off, staring up at the cathedral like tourists. Mrs Carter pointed at the tower, and Maisie knew that she had seen her. She retreated behind a buttress. Though she was further away than before, the men's voices carried in the still night air.

'Do you have anything else for me to do?' Mr Howarth's voice was almost pleading.

'Not at present.' Another pause. 'I shall be getting on my way.'

'But what about —'

'Your reward? I shall attend to that in due course. Good

evening, Jackal.'

'I thought it was you!' said Mrs Carter's loud, confident voice. 'I just said to Mr Carter, isn't that the gentleman from the train, the one with Mr Hamilton, and it is!' Slight pause. 'I'm terribly sorry if I've interrupted anything.'

'Not at all,' said Leopard, and Maisie could imagine his courtly half-bow. 'An old acquaintance of mine. We ran into each other by chance, and have made arrangements to meet properly tomorrow. Goodnight.'

'Goodnight,' said Mr Howarth, but he didn't sound so sure.

'An old acquaintance?' said Mrs Carter, once Leopard's footsteps had died away. 'Didn't you say that you hadn't been to Calcutta before?'

'No, I know him from Bombay,' said Mr Howarth, a little too quickly.

'Oh, I see,' said Mrs Carter. 'So you came to visit the cathedral. It is wonderful, isn't it?'

'Yes,' said Mr Howarth, 'very wonderful. Now if you'll excuse me, I was just heading to my hotel —'

'I thought we'd bump into you at the reception,' said Mrs Carter. 'We found Miss Frobisher and Mr Hamilton, and a couple of other people from the train, but I didn't see you anywhere.'

'I had to leave early,' said Mr Howarth. 'Now if you don't mind —'

'But I do mind,' said Mrs Carter, still in the same genial voice. 'I'd like you to remain here until your friend has gone.' She pulled aside her bag to reveal her gun.

'What on earth do you think you're doing, madam?'

But Mr Howarth's voice lacked conviction.

'My job, Mr Howarth.' Mrs Carter raised her voice. 'Miss Frobisher, you may show yourself now.'

Maisie pulled her own gun from her bag and walked into view, keeping well back and hoping that she would not have to use it. Mr Howarth stared at her as though he had seen a ghost. 'Good evening, Mr Howarth . . . or should I say Jackal?'

'Did you enjoy the gentlemen's conversation, Miss Frobisher?' asked Mrs Carter, her eyes never leaving Mr Howarth's face.

'Oh yes, it was very entertaining,' Maisie replied. 'I particularly enjoyed the bit he invented about me.'

'Telling lies?' Mrs Carter frowned. 'That's naughty. What do you have to say for yourself, Mr Howarth?'

Mr Howarth cleared his throat, and raised the back of his hand to his mouth as if suppressing a cough. He wore a signet ring on that hand, and Maisie saw his teeth pull at the seal —

'No!' she exclaimed, pulling his hand away from his mouth. But it was too late. Mr Howarth had already swallowed whatever was hidden in the ring, and grinned with evil mischief. 'You can't make me talk now,' he said.

'Oh yes I can,' said Mrs Carter. 'Randolph, cover me.' She handed her gun to Maisie, then pinched Mr Howarth's nose and stuck two fingers down his throat. He retched, and gasped, and struggled, but Mrs Carter held him until he coughed up a small white pill. 'How revolting,' she said, releasing him and wiping her hands on her handkerchief. 'Just like a disobedient puppy.' She looked at him, and there was no mercy in that look. 'Mr Howarth, I'll ask you to accompany us quietly to our carriage, since I don't propose to handcuff you in the middle of Calcutta.'

'What's the alternative?' said Mr Howarth, hoarsely.

'If you do try to run, I shall shoot you in the back like the coward you are. Off we go.'

With Mr Howarth leading, they proceeded towards the carriage, where Inspector Hamilton was waiting.

'Good evening, Mr Hamilton,' said Mrs Carter. 'All satisfactory?'

'I think so, Mrs Carter,' he replied. 'Oh, and it's Inspector, by the way.' Mr Howarth shot him a look of utter loathing, and muttered something under his breath.

'I do apologise, Inspector,' said Mrs Carter. 'Mr Howarth is rather grumpy and I can't think why. I propose we take him to the viceroy, and let him sort it out.'

'What a good idea,' said Inspector Hamilton with a smile. 'After all, Howarth, you've always wanted to meet the viceroy, haven't you?'

CHAPTER 20

'The reception is over,' said the attendant. 'It finished half an hour ago.' He flicked a disapproving glance at Maisie, who realised that Mrs Carter's cloak had fallen open and was displaying her once-beautiful muslin dress in its now stained and crumpled glory. She wrapped the cloak tightly round herself, and folded her arms.

'We are not here for the reception,' said Mrs Carter. She rummaged in her bag and extracted a card case, which she opened and showed to the attendant.

His eyes widened, and he gasped. 'Oh, I'm so sorry, I didn't —'

'People generally don't,' said Mrs Carter. 'Now if you wouldn't mind admitting us, the viceroy will be very interested in what we have to say. I don't mind waiting,' she added, reasonably.

With many bows and apologies the attendant saw them

through the door and into a small antechamber off the hall. 'I'll go and find the viceroy,' he gabbled.

'Please do,' said Mrs Carter. 'Oh, and put someone outside the door, too. Just in case.'

Maisie glanced into the mirror over the mantelpiece as she passed, and wished she hadn't. Her hair was pulled straight back from her face in a most unbecoming manner, apart from a stray piece which had escaped the hairpins and bobbed in the middle of her forehead. Her face was tear-stained and grubby, and her dress would never be the same again. 'Oh dear,' she murmured. 'This isn't how I thought it would be.'

'You sit there,' Mrs Carter instructed Mr Howarth, indicating the chair furthest from the door and casually laying her gun on her knee. 'What was that, my dear?' she said to Maisie.

'I didn't think, when I met the Viceroy of India, that I would look such a mess,' said Maisie.

'It could be much worse,' said Mrs Carter, eyeing Mr Howarth, whose shirt-front bore several marks of Mrs Carter's handling of the pill incident. 'I've come in here splattered with blood before now. Not that I'd recommend it.'

'So what *do* you —'

'Later, dear.'

The door creaked open and the attendant appeared. 'The viceroy is on his way.' He bowed and retreated.

'Do sit down, Miss Frobisher, you're making the place look untidy,' said Mrs Carter. 'There is room next to the inspector.'

Maisie obeyed, and the inspector put a careful arm around her. 'Are you all right, Maisie?'

Maisie sighed, and sat up straight. 'Yes, but . . . I suppose I'm tired. This morning on the train seems a long time ago.' Her stomach growled in response.

'Please stand for the viceroy!' cried a voice, and everyone got to their feet. The viceroy came in; but a rather different viceroy to the one at the reception, for his tie was gone, his collar removed, and he wore a pair of slippers.

'This is a pretty show!' he exclaimed, smiling. 'Mrs Carter, my servant told me that you were here, but he did not mention the rest of your party. I apologise for my state of dress. And do sit, all of you.' He seated himself in the only vacant chair. 'So, what brings you here?'

'I am afraid, Your Excellency, that this is not a pleasant matter,' said Mrs Carter. 'Two of my friends have managed to uncover treachery in the service, and this man —' She waved a hand at Mr Howarth, 'is part of it.'

'Always on a busy night,' groaned Lord Strathcairn. 'Very well, what's been going on?'

'Mr Howarth invited me to a meeting and took an important document from me,' said Maisie, astonished at her own boldness. 'The document was a false one procured for me by Lord Montgomery, the governor of Bombay.'

Mr Howarth gasped. 'Quiet, you,' said Mr Carter. 'Carry on, Miss Frobisher.'

'He then pretended that he had set the meeting up to catch me out as a traitor, and locked me in a tomb with Inspector Hamilton, whom his men had knocked unconscious at the scene. Mr and Mrs Carter rescued us, and we followed Mr Howarth to St Paul's Cathedral, where he gave the document to a man named Leopard. Mrs Carter apprehended him, and — and here we are.' Maisie closed her mouth, feeling that she had perhaps never spoken such a jumble of nonsense in her whole life.

The viceroy looked puzzled. 'Mrs Carter, can you confirm this?'

'To the best of my knowledge, I can.' Mrs Carter shot a scornful glance at Mr Howarth. 'He tried to kill himself, but we soon put a stop to that, and I daresay you will be able to get some sense out of him.'

'Howarth…' the viceroy said, then scrutinised Mr Howarth, his nose wrinkled. 'Any relation to Howarth, the Commissioner in Assam?'

'He is my uncle,' said Mr Howarth, studying his shoes.

'And there was Howarth, the Resident in Hyderabad…'

Mr Howarth's gaze could not have sunk any lower. 'He — he was my father.'

'I see,' said the viceroy. 'And this is how you choose to carry on the family tradition.'

'That's why I took the pill,' said Mr Howarth. 'Anything, rather than knowing my family knew.'

'Not behaving in such a manner in the first place would have been far better,' said Lord Strathcairn drily. 'But here we are.' He scrutinised Mr Howarth's face. 'My proposition is this: if you tell me exactly what happened, and everything you know, I shall see to it that your disgrace is not made public, and you can be quietly swept under the carpet. I am sure you can imagine the alternative.'

Mr Howarth nodded so hard that Maisie feared he might break his neck. 'Anything but that,' he croaked. He was sweating profusely. 'I'll tell you everything.'

'I don't need everything just yet,' said the viceroy. 'For one thing, after two hours of being sociable, I don't think I could bear it. First of all, is what Miss —' He looked at Maisie for guidance.

'Frobisher, Your Excellency,' Maisie supplied.

'Thank you,' said the viceroy. 'Is what Miss Frobisher said broadly true?'

'I am ashamed to say that it is, Your Excellency,' said Mr Howarth. He seemed ready to keel over.

'I am forgetting my manners,' said the viceroy. He clapped his hands, and a servant appeared in the doorway. 'Tea for our guests, please, and whatever refreshments we have left.' He turned back to Mr Howarth. 'Who is Leopard?'

'I don't know,' said Mr Howarth.

The viceroy's brow lowered. 'What did I just say?'

'I don't!' Mr Howarth cried. 'I honestly don't.'

'I think he is telling the truth,' said Mrs Carter. 'When I — happened upon him with Leopard, neither used each other's name. I suspect that each link in the chain knows the bare minimum they need to do their job.'

'That's right,' said Mr Howarth, with a look of gratitude at Mrs Carter. 'All I had was an instruction of where to send messages, and the name Leopard. The only person I've ever met is the one who recruited me.'

'And who was that?' asked the viceroy. 'Was it someone that you worked with?'

'No,' said Mr Howarth, 'or at least, not for long. He was an official passing through on his way to Simla. A man called Saunders; Lieutenant Saunders.'

'A young man, fair-haired and slight, with a scar on his forehead?' the viceroy asked.

'That's him!' exclaimed Mr Howarth, half-getting up in his excitement. 'That's the man!'

'And how did he — interest you in the work?' asked the viceroy. 'How long have you been engaged in these activities?'

'Two years,' said Mr Howarth. 'Lieutenant Saunders came to some events at Government House, and also spent time with us in the secretariat — to see how things were done, he said, as he was on his way to a new post. He was a good listener, and he would often join us for a drink at the end of the day, or on a ride out. We became friendly, and he said he had noticed how hard I worked, and how I was passed over, and he said it was a shame. And I listened to him.' He covered his face with his hands.

'Go on,' said the viceroy. 'That's an order.'

'He hinted that there were ways I could be better rewarded, and keep my position in the service. Nothing dangerous, you understand. Nothing harmful, merely a few — convenient actions.' He swallowed. 'At first it was merely a figure altered, or a letter not sent. He was fulsome with his praise, and said I was ready for more responsibility.' He gazed miserably at the governor. 'It was so long since anyone had praised me.'

'After a few weeks Lieutenant Saunders went on his way, and perhaps three months later a letter came —

printed, not written — instructing me what to do next. I obeyed, and the rewards came swiftly. It was like a game, an addictive game, to pay back the people who ignored me. I falsified figures, I sent anonymous letters, I spread misinformation.' He blinked, as if he could barely believe it himself, then took a deep breath and continued.

'I plucked up courage and suggested that Miss Jeroboam could be a useful operative, and I was rewarded for that too. I was tasked with meeting her in Bombay, then conveying the document she would give me to Leopard. But she did not come, and I read the report of her death. There was no mention of a missing document. Had it been hushed up? I didn't know, and could hardly ask. I spent time getting the Smythes to trust me, and I noted that Mrs Smythe in particular spoke slightingly of Miss Frobisher.' He glanced at Maisie, shamefaced. 'From what she said, I gathered that Miss Frobisher had been friends with Miss Jeroboam, and that she was, perhaps, not to be trusted. So I fastened on Miss Frobisher as a possible lead.'

I could wring Mrs Smythe's neck, Maisie fumed, but Mr Howarth was speaking again.

'I had seen a message from Leopard in the *Bombay Telegraph*, but there was no reply. I placed further messages in the paper, also supposedly from Leopard. I had already made sure that Miss Frobisher was invited to a dinner at Government House, and taken the opportunity to instruct her to wear white muslin, to see if she was biddable. She was.' He coughed nervously.

'I nurtured Mrs Smythe's dislike of Miss Frobisher to the point where she would willingly repeat the rumours I planted in her mind, and cut Miss Frobisher off from Bombay society. Then I received an answer to one of my messages, signed *Panther*, and I knew that the trail was not cold. I sent Miss Frobisher a ticket to Calcutta. I had no idea what I would do with her when we met; my focus was solely on getting the document and conveying it to Leopard.' He paused, choosing his words. 'I had not bargained for Mr Hamilton being sent on an assignment to Calcutta on the same train, and when I found him in Miss Frobisher's cabin I realised my plans would have to change. I had a Calcutta guidebook with me, and I arranged a note inviting Miss Frobisher to a deserted cemetery. I knew that Mr Hamilton would accompany her; and I paid some thugs to deal with him.'

'And the rest we know,' said Mrs Carter. Her gaze rested on him. 'If you had used half this ingenuity in discharging your duties, Mr Howarth, you would probably occupy a position to be proud of now.'

'I did,' said Mr Howarth, 'but it made no difference.'

The door opened and an attendant wheeled in a trolley with a tea urn and cups, and plates of snacks and canapés. 'Very good,' said the viceroy. 'I'm sorry to ask for yet another thing, but do you think that you could summon two or three stout policemen? We have a small matter to deal with.' The attendant stared at the viceroy for a moment, then bowed and withdrew.

Mrs Carter began filling plates with a selection of delicacies and passing them around. 'Eat up, Mr Howarth,' she said, passing a plate to him. 'You probably won't get food as nice as this for quite some time.'

Maisie accepted a plate of food and a cup of tea with plenty of sugar. She glanced at the inspector, who was doing his best to eat a bhaji carefully. He caught her eye mid-bite, and winked. 'Do eat, Maisie,' he said, when he was in a position to speak. 'I could scarcely hear Mr Howarth's enthralling narrative for your stomach churning.'

Maisie glared at him. 'Thank you for your concern,' she said. He nudged her gently, and Maisie bit her lip to keep herself from giggling, then suddenly felt as if she might burst into tears. She bit into a samosa and chewed vigorously till the feeling had passed.

They ate in silence until the attendant knocked. 'The policemen are here, Your Excellency,' he said in an undertone.

'Send 'em in, please,' said the viceroy, and three policemen fitted in the narrow doorway as best they could. 'See that chap there?' he said, jerking a thumb in Mr Howarth's direction. 'I would like you to arrest him for — I'm not sure how to describe it, so let's say theft. Take him out through the back way, and lock him up at the nearest station. I'll send someone to explain in the morning.'

'I'll come quietly,' said Mr Howarth, rising and almost running towards the policemen.

'He's a willing one, Your Excellency,' said the nearest policeman, with approval. He took Mr Howarth's arm. 'This way, sir.' Their heavy boots thumped on the hall floor till a door closed, and they were silenced.

'I'm sure I shall understand it all in time,' said the viceroy. He studied Maisie and the inspector. 'So you are the young pair Montgomery warned me about?'

Maisie and the inspector exchanged glances. 'I think we are, Your Excellency,' said Inspector Hamilton. 'I believe Lord Montgomery recommended me for surveying work.'

'Did he, now,' said the viceroy. 'You're rather pale for a surveyor, if you don't mind me saying.'

'I'm a police inspector,' said Inspector Hamilton. 'I came out on the same ship as Miss Frobisher, to look into the information leaks in Bombay.'

'So Montgomery hired both of you, did he?'

'Not exactly,' said Maisie. 'I was just travelling, and — I got involved.'

'She has a habit of doing that, Your Excellency,' said Inspector Hamilton, and Maisie glared at him again.

'I see,' said Lord Strathcairn. 'Well, it has paid off this time. And you, Mrs Carter?'

'It was nothing to do with me,' Mrs Carter said. 'Randolph had been called out here to do some work, and I was merely accompanying him as my wifely duty. But on the train I happened to be sitting at the same dinner table as Miss Frobisher, and who else should be there but Ainsley.'

'Ainsley?' cried Maisie. 'You know him?'

'Of course I know him,' said Mrs Carter. 'He is one of mine, or was. Anyway, one evening he asked for a quiet word. Turns out that Lord Montgomery knew he'd be on the train, and asked him to make sure that nothing happened to Miss Frobisher, since she was engaged in a job for him. Ainsley had tried to drop a hint that he was on her side, but Miss Frobisher took it the wrong way and spent the rest of the journey avoiding him. "As another woman she might listen to you, Mrs C," he said. So I kept watch and sure enough, off this pair slipped from your reception this evening.' She sighed. 'I wish we could have got Leopard too, but with four of us, one injured and one not used to firearms, I decided the best course of action was to get a good look at him and let him go. But we asked Inspector Hamilton to lurk nearby and follow Leopard as far as he reasonably could.'

'I managed to keep him in sight until the main road,' said the inspector. 'He hailed a rickshaw, and when I went past I heard him say, "Chowringhee Road, please."'

'That doesn't tell us much,' said Mrs Carter. 'It's the equivalent of going to the high street.'

'What was he like, this Leopard?' asked the viceroy.

'Pale linen suit, good quality, white shirt, tan shoes, well polished,' sad the inspector. 'Tall, broad inclining to plump, dark hair with grey at the sides, and olive skin.'

'Round brown eyes, a slightly hooked nose, a weak chin, and a mole at the corner of his left eye,' added Mrs Carter.

'And an unusual voice,' said Maisie. 'He sounded as if he could hypnotise you, if he wanted.'

Lord Strathcairn walked to the sofa where Maisie and the inspector were sitting. 'Look at this photograph,' he said, pointing to a frame above them. 'The second row, in particular.'

Maisie scanned the photograph, which showed a large group of people standing on the steps of Government House. She focused on the second row. Surely —

'That's him,' said Mr Carter. 'Fifth from the left.'

'I agree,' said Mrs Carter. 'And Randolph is good with faces.'

'I think so too,' Maisie and the inspector said together, and exchanged glances.

'Who is he?' asked Mrs Carter.

'I won't tell you his name just yet,' said the viceroy. 'He is a businessman, but not someone with enough power to make me think he is a major player in this game. There will be someone behind him, and, no doubt, someone behind them. But it is a very good beginning.'

'This Lieutenant Saunders Mr Howarth spoke of,' said Mrs Carter, 'I don't think I've encountered him.'

'I don't suppose you have,' said the viceroy. 'He was a fairly minor official.'

'Was?' said Inspector Hamilton.

Lord Strathcairn looked at the inspector, and his gaze did not waver. 'He died of fever that summer up in Simla,' he said quietly. 'So whoever has been issuing orders to Howarth, it wasn't him.'

He was silent for a moment, but then he came to himself with a start. 'It is getting late, and we are all tired. I suggest we get some rest.' He eyed Maisie and the inspector. 'Perhaps a hot bath too, and then I suggest we reconvene tomorrow morning.'

**

The Carters dropped the inspector off before driving to Maisie's hotel. 'Your inspector needs his sleep,' Mrs Carter said firmly.

'He isn't my inspector,' said Maisie.

'Isn't he?' Mrs Carter laughed. 'You could have fooled me. Anyway, do as the viceroy says. A bath and a good rest, and you'll be right as rain in the morning once you've had a proper breakfast.'

'But you still haven't told me what you —'

'It'll keep,' said Mrs Carter. 'Off you go.'

Maisie soaked in the bath till her fingertips were wrinkly, then sat in the armchair in her dressing-gown. *How can I possibly sleep? I've been locked in a tomb, rescued by a sort of super-spy, helped to arrest a traitor, and had supper with the Viceroy of India.* Her gaze lighted on her muslin frock, which she had left on her bedroom floor as past hope, and she burst out laughing. *And I did it all in that dress!* She smiled fondly at it, and knew that, no matter how dirty and torn it was, she would never, ever throw it away.

CHAPTER 21

'I could get used to this,' said Maisie, as they swayed along the path, and the outskirts of Calcutta undulated gently around them.

'So could I,' said Inspector Hamilton. 'It certainly beats pen-pushing in a hot office and being patronised by Mr Howarth.'

'That isn't likely to happen again in a hurry,' said Maisie. 'Oh, we are slowing down.' She peered through the hangings of the howdah. 'I think we're stopping.'

The moon was high in the sky, so that even the blades of grass stood out, and the trees cast eerie shadows. Maisie shivered, remembering another bright moonlit night not so long ago.

The inspector leaned over and put an arm round her. 'Try not to think about it, Maisie,' he said. 'I know it was horrible being trapped in that tomb —'

'It wasn't that so much,' said Maisie. 'I knew you weren't dead, but I didn't know if you would come round, or what state you'd be in . . . or anything.' She lifted her chin and kissed him. 'Now you've made me do that, and probably the whole party have seen.'

'Never mind them,' said the inspector. 'Can't we carry on pretending we're married?'

'I'm sure some of them think we're engaged,' said Maisie. 'Otherwise they'd never let us share an elephant.'

'Isn't that just because we're an elephant short?' said the inspector.

'And why are we an elephant short?' demanded Maisie. 'Answer me that.'

The inspector laughed. 'You see skulduggery everywhere, Maisie.' He leaned towards her again, but the elephant chose that moment to kneel, and he had to grip the pole of the howdah to keep himself from being thrown out.

Once everyone was safely down, the mahouts busied themselves laying rugs and unpacking picnic baskets. 'Come and help, you two,' said Mrs Carter, sailing by with a folding stool and a corkscrew. 'You'll never get a meal if you stand there chatting.'

'I'm still not quite sure what she does,' said Maisie out of the side of her mouth. Was she imagining it, or did Mrs Carter hesitate a fraction as she spoke, then move on? She remembered the inspector's comment about skulduggery, and dismissed it, but another determined, daring woman came into her mind; a woman who had chosen a different path from Mrs Carter, and ended up dead because of it. A wave of regret broke over her for Miss Jeroboam, who could have been a good friend and an ally, and now never could.

'I think she likes it that way,' said the inspector, 'but she is clearly very important.'

'Yes, she is,' said Maisie, watching Mrs Carter direct the mahouts and her husband. 'She asked if I'd be interested in working with her again,' she added, as casually as she could.

The inspector stared. 'What did you say?'

'I said I would.'

'Oh.' He picked up a picnic basket.

Maisie picked up a basket too and walked alongside him. 'You don't mind, do you?'

He was quiet for a moment. 'I don't know if I'm allowed to mind or not,' he said. 'It isn't as if we're married.'

'Would you like to be?' Maisie asked, with a smile.

'I really don't know.' Inspector Hamilton frowned. 'You accept invitations from strange men to meet in cemeteries, you don't sing as well as I would wish, and you can be untidy in your personal appearance…'

Maisie wondered whether swinging a picnic basket at his head would damage the food or attract attention, and concluded reluctantly that it would. 'You've made your point,' she said, and walked on.

'But on the other hand,' the inspector continued, 'you join me on adventures, and you looked after me when I was knocked out. And sometimes, like today, you even scrub up quite well.'

'So do you,' said Maisie. 'Although I do rather regret those breeches that you had in Bombay. Not to mention the riding boots.'

'I could send for the boots,' he replied. 'Would you like me to?'

'I do like a gentleman to be well shod,' said Maisie.

Somehow they had managed to take a wrong fork in the path, and while they could hear the rest of the party chattering not far away, they could not see them. 'The viceroy asked if I'd like to stay,' said Inspector Hamilton. 'Now that Howarth's been winkled out of Bombay, he considers that there is more for me to do here.'

Maisie moved towards him. 'What do you think?'

'I'm not sure,' said the inspector. 'I was supposed to be working for Lord Montgomery, and I feel disloyal for leaving him. But there will be plenty to do in Calcutta.'

Maisie sighed. 'More people to make acquaintance with,' she said. 'Knowing my luck, more people to offend.'

'No one will be offended with you in Bombay now,' said the inspector, laughing. 'The governor will see to that.'

'Lady Montgomery did write a very kind letter,' said Maisie. 'And I can't say I regret the departure of the Smythes.'

Mr Howarth's account of how he had manipulated Mrs Smythe, coupled with the intelligence that the inspector and Maisie had shared privately with Lord Strathcairn, had led him to conclude that Mr Smythe's health was not best suited to the Indian climate, and to write a letter of recommendation accordingly. 'Somewhere bracing,' he said. 'There is an official in Sweden who I believe is ready to move on to greater things. I shall make the suggestion.'

A small table stood in the corner of the viceroy's study, with a chessboard laid ready. Maisie had imagined Lord Strathcairn moving the pieces round the board, threatening and capturing and removing, and shivered despite the humid atmosphere.

'So I shall be popular in Bombay again,' she said. 'Is that enough incentive to return?'

'You could resume your dalliance with Mr Mandeville,' said the inspector.

'I could,' said Maisie. 'After all, it isn't as if there is anyone else. I should move quickly, before he gets snapped up by one of the Darlings.'

'That's a point,' said Inspector Hamilton. 'I could reappear in Bombay, splendiferous in my riding boots and breeches, and carry off one of the Darlings.' He looked at Maisie, and the corner of his mouth curled up. 'Or…'

'Or…?' said Maisie.

He took a step towards her, then remembered that he was still holding a picnic basket, and put it down. He took her free hand. 'Maisie, will you marry me?'

'*What?*' said Maisie.

'You heard me,' he murmured. 'Will you do me the honour of becoming my wife?'

Maisie stared at him, completely overwhelmed. 'Aren't you supposed to kneel?'

He glanced at his linen trousers. 'And have everyone know what I've been doing?'

'Yes!' said Maisie happily.

The inspector sighed. 'I haven't a ring with me, you know. I didn't plan this.'

'Should I marry someone so unprepared?' whispered Maisie.

'And should I marry someone so demanding?' he whispered back, and kissed her.

A rustle of leaves made them look up. Mrs Carter was standing perhaps ten feet away, with an exasperated expression on her face. 'There you are!' she exclaimed. 'Are you coming to this picnic? What do you think you're doing?'

Maisie and the inspector burst out laughing. 'I couldn't possibly say, Mrs Carter,' said Maisie, 'for I don't think we know what we're doing at all.'

'I thought as much,' said Mrs Carter. 'Now do come along, before the food goes.' She swished through the grass, and Maisie and the inspector followed; but they stole another kiss first.

ACKNOWLEDGEMENTS

As ever, my first thanks go to my beta readers — Carol Bissett, Ruth Cunliffe, Mike Jackson and Stephen Lenhardt, who did a brilliant job. I'm also amazed that, having alpha-read the first draft of *All At Sea*, my fellow-author Paula Harmon offered to do it again!

A further thank you to John Croall, who proofread the manuscript and in this instance also acted as lighting advisor. It's just as well that he did, or the polo match would have been conducted in very dim light! Any errors which remain are of course my responsibility.

A thank-you as big as an Indian elephant goes to my husband Stephen Lenhardt for his considerable support. Not only does he beta-read for me, but he also regularly asks me how many people I've murdered when he gets home. Somehow he always manages to tell me off, either for murdering people, not murdering them, or because of what I've let Maisie and Inspector Hamilton get up to.

A fair bit of research went into this book. These are the books I found most useful:

Rudyard Kipling, *Plain Tales from the Hills* and *Kim*

Pat Barr, *The Memsahibs: The Women of Victorian India*

David Gilmour, *The Ruling Caste* — this account of the Indian Civil Service was absolutely indispensable.

Something I hadn't realised before I began researching British India during the nineteenth century was how very separate the British and the Indians were, certainly in terms of their social lives. At times it wasn't comfortable to write, but I felt it would be wrong, and misleading, to produce a narrative inauthentic to the period.

I've done my best to include places and buildings which would have been in Mumbai and Kolkata at the time; but all characters are entirely fictitious. Again, as in *All At Sea,* I've used the place names that were current at the time, so Bombay instead of Mumbai, Calcutta instead of Kolkata, etc.

And finally, thank you for reading! I hope you've enjoyed Maisie's latest adventure, and if you could leave a short review or star rating on Amazon or Goodreads, I'd appreciate it very much.

Font and image credits

Fonts:

Title font: Limelight by Eben Sorkin: https://

www.fontsquirrel.com/fonts/limelight. License — SIL Open Font License v.1.10: http://scripts.sil.org/OFL

Script font: Alex Brush by TypeSETit: https://www.fontsquirrel.com/fonts/alex-brush. License — SIL Open Font License v.1.10: http://scripts.sil.org/OFL

Graphics:

Indian background (edited to remove lettering and partially recoloured): Background vector createdmby freepik: https://www.freepik.com/free-vector/beautiful-indian-independence-day-background_2420732.htm

Female silhouette: Gala dresses silhouettes vector created by renata s: https://www.freepik.com/free-vector/gala-dresses-silhouettes_1209311.htm

Male silhouette: Adult silhouettes background vector created by pikisuperstar: https://www.freepik.com/free-vector/adult-people-silhouettes-background_4130489.htm

Series frame: frame vector created by alvaro_cabrera: https://www.freepik.com/free-vector/eight-ornamental-frames_961366.htm

Maisie cameo (modified and recoloured): Vintage vector created by freepik: https://www.freepik.com/free-vector/beautiful-woman-silhouette_811219.htm

Elephant chapter vignette: Background vector created by brgfx: https://www.freepik.com/free-vector/set-silhouette-exotic-animals_3888365.htm

Cover created using GIMP image editor: www.gimp.org.

ABOUT LIZ HEDGECOCK

Liz Hedgecock grew up in London, England, did an English degree, and then took forever to start writing. After several years working in the National Health Service, some short stories crept into the world. A few even won prizes. Then the stories started to grow longer…

Now Liz travels between the nineteenth and twenty-first centuries, murdering people. To be fair, she does usually clean up after herself.

Liz's reimaginings of Sherlock Holmes, her Pippa Parker cozy mystery series, and the Caster & Fleet Victorian mystery series (written with Paula Harmon), are available in ebook and paperback.

Liz lives in Cheshire with her husband and two sons, and when she's not writing or child-wrangling you can usually find her reading, messing about on Twitter, or cooing over stuff in museums and art galleries. That's her story, anyway, and she's sticking to it.

Website/blog: http://lizhedgecock.wordpress.com
Facebook: http://www.facebook.com/lizhedgecockwrites
Twitter: http://twitter.com/lizhedgecock
Goodreads: https://www.goodreads.com/lizhedgecock

BOOKS BY LIZ HEDGECOCK

Short stories
The Secret Notebook of Sherlock Holmes
Bitesize
The Adventure of the Scarlet Rosebud

Halloween Sherlock series (novelettes)
The Case of the Snow-White Lady
Sherlock Holmes and the Deathly Fog
The Case of the Curious Cabinet

Sherlock & Jack series (novellas)
A Jar Of Thursday
Something Blue
A Phoenix Rises

Mrs Hudson & Sherlock Holmes series (novels)
A House Of Mirrors
In Sherlock's Shadow

Pippa Parker Mysteries (novels)
Murder At The Playgroup
Murder In The Choir
A Fete Worse Than Death
Murder in the Meadow
The QWERTY Murders

Caster & Fleet Mysteries (with Paula Harmon)
The Case of the Black Tulips

The Case of the Runaway Client
The Case of the Deceased Clerk
The Case of the Masquerade Mob
The Case of the Fateful Legacy
The Case of the Crystal Kisses

Maisie Frobisher Mysteries (novels)
All At Sea
Off The Map (February 2020)
Gone To Ground (April 2020)

For children (with Zoe Harmon)
A Christmas Carrot

WHITE RHINO BOOKS

Printed in Poland
by Amazon Fulfillment
Poland Sp. z o.o., Wrocław